IN THE KEEP
OF TIME

by MARGARET J. ANDERSON

Cover by
LASZLO KUBINYI

SCHOLASTIC BOOK SERVICES

NEW YORK • TORONTO • LONDON • AUCKLAND • SYDNEY • TOKYO

For my Mother and Father
who know the magic of Smailholm Tower

Copyright © 1977 by Margaret Anderson. All rights reserved. This edition is published by Scholastic Book Services, a division of Scholastic Magazines, Inc., by arrangement with Alfred A. Knopf, Inc.

12 11 10 9 8 7 6 5 4 3 2 1   2   8 9/7 0 1 2 3/8
                                                    06
Printed in the U. S. A.

IN THE KEEP OF TIME

1

A sudden shower of rain washed the tall, straight walls of Smailholm Tower, and then the sun shone with a silver light that picked out the red stone against the gray-black granite so that the simple building became a monument of beauty.

That was how it looked when the four Elliot children first saw it. Just as they tumbled out of the car a shaft of sunlight broke through the clouds and, for a moment, the children felt the magic in its shimmering walls. Then the sunshine faded, the stone grew dull, and three of the children turned their backs on the castle and trudged into

Smailholm Cottage to be introduced to their Great Aunt Grace.

Ollie, the youngest, stood for a little longer, gazing at the tower. She had been asleep when they arrived. Her face was flushed, her blond hair sticky, and her clothes rumpled. She had been dreaming about the castle, and it gave her a strange feeling to wake up and find that it was real.

Then, from inside the cottage, her mother called, "Ollie, come in and meet Aunt Grace."

She was their father's aunt, and very old. At least Ollie thought so. Her hair was thin and white and was twisted into tight little curls so that her scalp showed pink between the curls. Her face, brown and wrinkled, was dominated by a sharp nose and very blue eyes.

"Now, let me see," she said. "Andrew's the oldest, isn't he? But you're the tallest. Are you Elinor? Fancy letting your sister outgrow you like that, Andrew!"

Elinor blushed. She felt gangly. This last year she had been taller than any of her friends, but she knew that Andrew hated that sort of remark even more, and he had been against this visit from the start.

"Elinor shot up this last year," said Mrs. Elliot rather loudly. "Andrew will have a growing spurt soon."

They had heard that before, too.

"And the two little ones must be Ian and Olivia. I haven't seen them before, have I?" asked Aunt Grace.

"No, it was the year before Ian was born that you visited us in London," said Mr. Elliot. "Eight years ago, that must have been."

"Well, come and have your tea," said Aunt Grace. "You'll be hungry after the long drive."

They weren't hungry. They had stopped at a cafe just before they left the Motorway because Mrs. Elliot thought they had better not arrive at Aunt Grace's house famished in case she wasn't expecting them so early. However, they managed to do justice to the tea Aunt Grace had provided, and Olivia, or Ollie as the others called her, ate two cream cupcakes and was reaching for a third when her mother stopped her.

When Mr. Elliot was a boy he had spent all his holidays at Smailholm Cottage. He had helped on a neighbor's farm and had made a few friends in the village, but mostly he had hiked in the hills, fished in the river, and looked for birds' nests in the woods. He had loved those summers at Smailholm Cottage.

Now, living in London, he sometimes felt

guilty that his children never experienced the freedom that he had known. They were busy and happy and took classes in everything from making clay pots to gymnastics, but he still felt they were being cheated, spending their childhood in the city. So, when his firm proposed to send him to France for the summer, he suggested that Mrs. Elliot should go with him, and the children should spend the summer in Scotland with Aunt Grace.

"She's far too old for that responsibility," Mrs. Elliot had protested. "She couldn't look after four children."

"She's not *that* old," said Mr. Elliot. "And she has plenty of energy. Remember how she wore us out on that visit she paid us a few years ago? She was determined to see everything listed in that guide book she bought and had us visiting places in London we hadn't known existed. Besides, she wouldn't need to look after the children. After all, Andrew is twelve and Elinor eleven. It's time *they* took on some responsibility. They can look after themselves and keep an eye on the younger two."

"But just cooking and shopping for four children with appetites like theirs — that would be asking a lot of anyone!"

"Andrew and Elinor can do the cooking," interrupted her husband. "They'd see a need for it there. Here they let you do everything. And being out in the country would be so good for them. It's a marvelous place for children. There's a tower — I called it a castle — about a quarter of a mile from the house."

"What would they do there? They'd miss their friends."

"They'd have each other. When I was a boy I managed to have a great time just by myself. Think how they will enjoy it, all four of them."

Mrs. Elliot felt there was something wrong with her husband's logic and was surprised that he couldn't see it. The four Elliot children didn't spend much time together, but what time they did was spent arguing. Take the matter of television. Whenever one wanted to watch a program, there was always something on another channel that someone else wanted to see. Or food. They'd never find a kind of breakfast cereal to suit them all, and Aunt Grace would end up with a larder full of stale packets of Oatsios or Winky Stars or whatever these things were that they nagged for.

The Elliot children tended to side with

their mother on the subject of the holiday. Ian and Ollie liked the idea of a real castle to play in, but they didn't want to be bossed around by Andrew and Elinor all summer. Elinor thought the country sounded nice but she would miss her friend Susan and gymnastics lessons, and Andrew said he'd be bored.

But Mr. Elliot prevailed. Maybe it was the thought of a summer in France, or maybe it was the children's constant complaining, but Mrs. Elliot suddenly agreed with her husband that a visit to Aunt Grace's would be good for them. A summer in the country, with a castle at their back door, was just what the children needed.

Andrew still thought it would be boring.

When tea was over — Ollie managed to sneak a third cake — Mr. Elliot was pleased to hear Elinor and Andrew offer to do the dishes, and even Mrs. Elliot relaxed a little. She had been filled with last-minute misgivings at the thought of being parted from the children, but seeing Elinor and Andrew busy, Ian leaning comfortably against Aunt Grace's knee, and Ollie sprawled by the fire looking at a magazine, she was content. They would all manage.

Then it was time for the parents to leave. Mrs. Elliot hugged the children, and Ian clung to her, not wanting her to go. But Aunt Grace brought out her music box and let Ian wind it up. He liked the tinkly tune, but after Mr. and Mrs. Elliot had gone, the cottage seemed darker and very quiet. Even Elinor was close to tears.

"Why don't you all take a look at the castle," suggested Aunt Grace. "That was always the first thing your father did when he came to visit. You'll find the key in a box by the back door."

"By *your* back door?" asked Ollie.

"That's right, dear. I have the key. The castle belongs to the government, you know, and visitors have to come here to pick up the key if they want to look inside. You'll be surprised how many people come by for the key on a summer Sunday. You'll be able to show them around this year. There are days when I get tired of questions, but people *are* interested in the old keep. It has a sort of power over people, being so old and having seen so many come and go."

"Let's go take a look at it," said Andrew.

They had to wait until Elinor brushed her hair. Even before she brushed it, her brown hair was smooth and she looked tidier than the others. But they could see no point in getting washed and brushed up for a visit to an empty castle.

"Would you like to go with us, Aunt Grace?" Elinor asked politely, when she was ready. "Dad says you know all about the history of the castle."

"I would only tell you facts that you can find in any history book," answered Aunt Grace. "Go by yourselves, and perhaps — if you let it happen — you'll find out many things. The walls themselves have a story to tell."

Andrew shrugged and took the key from the box by the back door. Almost immediately, Ian and Ollie started squabbling about who should get to carry it. It was a big, important-looking key, but hardly worth such a fuss.

"Let Ollie carry it," Elinor suggested. "And then when we get to the castle Ian can turn the key in the lock and let us in."

Ollie ran ahead, waving the key and feeling important.

The sky had cleared, and the air was heavy with the sweet smell of hawthorn and damp earth. The country *is* nice, thought Elinor to herself, gazing all around at the fields and hedges and the rocky hillside where the castle stood. She didn't say it aloud, though. Andrew would only say it was boring.

The keep stood above them on a rise. A well-worn path wound around a small pond and up the rocky hillside. The final stretch of the path was steep and narrow, and the children were out of breath when they scrambled up to the door. Ollie pushed the key into the big keyhole, and Ian gave a wail.

"Let Ian turn it," Elinor said, and Ollie, rather reluctantly, allowed Ian to take the key.

The key turned quite easily, and the heavy door swung open. The four children pushed inside and then stood for a minute while their eyes adjusted to the darkness.

"Look, there's stairs right inside the wall," said Andrew. "Come on! Let's climb them."

The steps were worn and uneven, so they climbed slowly, feeling their way until they reached the first floor. Light filtered into the room through narrow windows, and the children, their eyes accustomed to the darkness of the stairs, could see quite clearly. They crowded into the room and stood looking up at its great height.

Suddenly a huge, black bird, perched on a high ledge, gave a hoarse croak and half-fluttering, half-falling, dropped from the height of the wall. It landed quite near Ollie's feet and gave one more harsh croak, two convulsive jerks, and then lay still.

"It's hurt," whispered Ian.

"What is it?" asked Elinor. "Don't touch it, Andrew," she added.

But Andrew picked it up, and the bird lay limp in his hands.

"I think it's dead," he said softly.

"How could it be?" asked Ian.

They questioned each other in uneasy whispers. They finally decided that the bird must have forced its way through the wire netting that covered the narrow windows and been unable to find its way back out. It had died of hunger. It was, in fact, little more than feathers and bones. The sound of their voices had been enough to scare the bird from its perch, but it had not had the strength to fly. Instead it had plummeted to its death.

"I wonder how long it had been trapped in here," said Andrew.

"Let's get out," said Elinor.

"But we have to bury it," protested Ollie.

"We could tell Aunt Grace," suggested Ian. "She could tell the government to take it away."

But Ollie took the dead bird gently in her

hands, and the others followed her down the stairs and outside.

"How can we dig a grave without a shovel?" asked Andrew.

"We'll put it in a rabbit hole," said Ollie.

"With a stone in front, like an Egyptian tomb," said Elinor. "But we must find a hole that doesn't look used. The rabbits wouldn't want a dead bird blocking their doorway."

Andrew finally found a hole that had no sign of rabbit droppings near it.

"This looks like an empty burrow," he said.

They pushed the dead bird inside and then stood for a moment in awkward silence. It seemed sort of sacrilegious to push the bird into the hole without any ceremony at all.

It was quite a relief when Ollie suddenly said, "In the name of the Father, the Son, and the Holy Ghost, Amen."

"That's that," said Andrew. "What will we do now?"

"Let's go back to the cottage," suggested Elinor.

Andrew locked the door and carried the key, and neither of the younger ones cared. They walked home in silence, and Aunt Grace was surprised to see them back so soon.

2

The next morning Andrew and Elinor did the breakfast dishes, though less eagerly than they had cleaned up the night before. Ian was pushing a little car along imaginary roads on the faded living room carpet. The worn patch in front of the fireplace was the parking lot, and he pushed at Ollie, who was sprawled on the carpet, reading.

"You're in my way!" he said. "Move!"

"Drive your car somewhere else."

Even though Ollie was only five-going-on-six (as she liked to say), she was always reading. She had learned to read before she was three, and now some of the books she read didn't even have pictures in them. Elinor and Andrew, if they thought about it at all, were rather proud of the way Ollie could read, but it annoyed Ian. He wasn't bad at reading — just about the same as most of the boys in his class — but Ollie made the books he could read look babyish, so he never read at home if he could help it.

"You're in my parking lot," he said. "Move!"

Ollie ignored him, as she was inclined to do when she was reading.

"You children should go out exploring," said Aunt Grace, coming into the living room. "It's a lovely morning. I remember how your father used to take a sandwich with him so that he didn't need to come home for lunch. There were so many places he had to visit."

"A picnic!" said Ollie, closing her book. "Come on and see if Andrew and Elinor will take us on a picnic."

Andrew and Elinor were not quite so enthusiastic as Ollie and Ian, but they did agree to help them make sandwiches. Aunt Grace found a jar of shrimp paste and spreading it thin, they made four sandwiches.

Once outside, the idea of the whole day before them was much less exciting than Aunt Grace imagined.

"Where should we go?" asked Elinor.

"Maybe we could go to the village and find some other kids," suggested Andrew.

"They're still in school here," Elinor said. "Aunt Grace said they don't get out for another week."

"Let's go back to the castle," suggested Ollie. "It's my turn to unlock the door."

"Not the castle," said Elinor, but Ian had already taken the key from the box.

"It looks different," he said.

He held out the key for the others to see, and it *was* different — more silver than black, and it seemed to glow with a faintly luminous haze. Perhaps it was only a trick of the summer sunshine.

"Let's pretend we're enemies sneaking up on the castle," suggested Ian, throwing himself down on the short grass. It was an excellent hillside for a sneak attack, with outcrops of rock and patches of gorse providing cover, but Andrew and Elinor weren't interested in playing.

"This is going to be the boringest summer," said Andrew, kicking a rock.

"You don't give it a chance," said Elinor.

"Are you enjoying yourself?" he challenged her.

"It's pretty around here," she answered.

"Pretty boring!"

When they reached the castle, Ollie and Ian were there ahead of them and were already arguing about who was to unlock the door.

"As if it mattered," said Andrew. "But let Ollie do it. You carried the key, Ian."

"It does shine," Ollie said, and fitted the key in the lock.

It turned easily, and the door swung open of its own accord. The children stepped inside the dark lower room.

"I want to go upstairs," said Ollie, pushing past the others. She felt her way up the narrow staircase. She didn't stop at the doorway of the first room but continued up the dark spiral stair with the others following close behind. They paused at the doorway of what had once been an upper room of the castle. There was now no floor, so they could not go beyond the doorway, which gaped high in the wall. Iron bars had been driven into the stone door frame to prevent the unwary or careless from falling.

"What's down there?" asked Ollie, lying down and sticking her head under the lowest bar.

There should have been enough light coming through the narrow windows for them to look down into the room where they had found the dead bird the day before, but everything was obscured by a strange, swirling mist with an eery luminous glow.

"It's like looking into a boiling pot," said Ian. "But cold," he added and shivered.

"Or thick fog," said Elinor.

"But it wasn't foggy outside," said Andrew.

They pushed closer, and Ollie — who always had to find out about everything — wriggled farther under the bar and snatched at the fog.

"Look out," said Andrew, for it seemed that the fog was trying to snatch at her.

Ollie leaned even farther, and a swirling cloud rose up to meet her. Andrew tried to hold her back, but she was pulled from his grasp. Ian and Elinor, gazing in fascination at the mist, seemed unaware of Ollie's danger. She hovered for a second above the blanket of mist, and then it parted and she was drawn down into it. She was completely hidden from them, and they saw only swirling shapes.

"She was dragged down into the fog," said Andrew in horror. "She must have fallen into the downstairs room. We've got to find her. Come on!"

Elinor and Ian roused themselves and followed Andrew down the stairs. They reached the doorway of the lower level, fearing that they would find Ollie lying on the floor, limp and stricken, just as they had found the bird the day before.

But at the doorway they stopped, transfixed. It was like that first moment in a theater when the curtain parts and the audience is transported to another place and time.

They stood riveted by the scene before them.

A fire was burning in the hearth, a big fire, and some sort of meat was broiling over it on a spit. Smoke, thick with the smell of grease, billowed into the room. On the walls were hangings of coarse woven fabric, and the floor was strewn with rushes. A candle flickered and guttered in a niche in the wall. The only furniture in the room was a heavy oak table, set with wooden bowls, and benches beside it. Two people, like actors on the stage, sat by the fire. A woman was teasing out the wool of what seemed to be a sheepskin, and a fair-haired child, wearing a tunic of coarse cloth, was idly plaiting rushes from the floor.

The child turned and looked in the direction of the children, and they gasped with astonishment, for the hair and features surely belonged to Ollie. How had she, in these few seconds, been transformed into this other child?

"Ollie," said Elinor, advancing into the room.

Andrew, Elinor, and Ian were no longer the audience, separated from the stage by footlights. They had become part of the action of the play.

"Ollie!" said Elinor again.

But Ollie turned and scuttled across the floor and hid herself in the skirts of the woman who jumped up and turned in their direction. She was incredibly ugly. Her mouth was distorted by a harelip, and her eyes moved in independent directions so that it was hard to tell where she was looking.

She spoke to them in a low, slurred voice. They could not understand her words, but there was no mistaking her meaning, for she picked up a huge meat cleaver and came toward them brandishing it.

They made for the doorway and clattered down the dark spiral staircase, tripping and bumping one another in their haste. Andrew stopped abruptly on the bottom step because the lower room seemed to be full of dark, moving shapes, and the air was heavy with the smell of cows and hay.

18

"There are animals in here," he said nervously.

Then they heard the harsh shouts of the woman as she came down the stairs after them. Taking Ian's hand in his, Andrew pushed between the softly lowing cows. The feel of their coarse hides and hot snuffling breath frightened him as much as the angry woman.

He reached the big door and dragged it open but was surprised and confused to find that it was pitch dark outside.

"Come on, Ian," he said, jerking his brother's arm, and together they ran, stumbling over the rough ground, followed by Elinor.

Andrew ran in what he hoped was the direction of Aunt Grace's cottage and, for a moment, he was reassured when he noticed the glimmer of the pond. Then the moon broke from behind a cloud and he saw a cluster of small thatched huts grouped beside the pond. Beyond that were the woods. The whole landscape was altered, and Aunt Grace's cottage was no longer part of it.

With a rising feeling of panic, Andrew looked for a place to hide. He dodged behind the last hut and saw that the door was just an animal skin, fastened to the lintel, hanging down over the entrance. Cautiously he pushed his way inside, followed by Ian and Elinor, and then let the skin fall back into place. It was completely dark.

"Where are we?" whispered Elinor.

Andrew did not answer. He was concentrating on a faint sound that seemed to come from farther inside the hut — a slight scratching of one stone against another. Then a tiny spark glowed in the darkness.

"So you have come," said a low voice.

"Let's get out of here," said Andrew, nervously pushing Elinor back to the doorway.

"You need not fear! I knew of your coming. To run from me will only cause great evil."

A small candle was lit and, by its flickering light, the children saw that the speaker was a very old woman. The wavering flame cast odd, leaping shadows, giving the impression of hollow cheeks, heavy eyebrows, and a huge beaked nose. The face was etched with a thousand wrinkles and seemed as old as time itself.

"So you have come," she repeated softly. "Step into the circle of light so I may see you."

The children moved obediently forward.

They were afraid, desperately afraid, but to turn and run was unthinkable. They were held by the power of the old woman.

She looked at them steadily, as if memorizing every feature, and then said, "It was foretold that four would come. Where is the other, and where is the silver key?"

Elinor shivered. The idea that this frightening woman had actually known of their coming added a new element of mystery and fear. "Ollie came with us," she whispered. "But a woman has her up at the keep."

"What woman?"

Ian spoke up. "An ugly woman," he said. "Her mouth is real wide, and her eyes look two ways."

Elinor was horrified and nudged Ian so hard that he stumbled forward. He could surely have found a more tactful description.

But the old woman only nodded and said, "That would be Muckle-mooth* Meg. I will go up to the keep and fetch the other one here."

She reached for a hooded cloak and wrapped it around herself.

"Stay here until I return."

She pushed aside the skin door and stepped

---

* Big mouth

out into the night, leaving the children alone in the darkness.

"Now's our chance," said Andrew. "Let's get out of here."

"Where are we?" asked Elinor. She was close to tears. "And what about Ollie? What has happened to us?"

"I think it was the key," said Ian. He sounded far less disturbed than the others. "I told you it looked different today."

"But how did we get here?"

"We unlocked the past," said Ian.

"That's impossible," said Andrew.

They stood together in the darkness, puzzling over their bewildered thoughts.

"That strange old woman said something about the key, too," said Andrew at last. "What happened to it?"

"Ollie unlocked the door," Ian answered. "And I think she left the key in the lock."

"Then the old woman will find it," said Andrew. "I wish we had it. Maybe we need it to get back."

"What will we do?" wailed Elinor.

"I'm going to try and get the key," said Andrew. "Perhaps I can still get up there ahead of her."

"Let's all go," said Elinor.

"No," said Andrew. "I'll come right back, but I stand a better chance alone."

It wasn't bravery that prompted Andrew to go and look for the key. It was simply that he couldn't stand still, confined in the hut, with so many questions whirling in his brain. However, his departure left Elinor more frightened than ever. The four of them never did do things together, but this losing first one, and then another, was unnerving. She reached for Ian's hand in the darkness in an unusual gesture of friendliness. "We'll just wait here," she said, "but I hope Andrew gets back before the old woman does. She might be angry with us if she found him gone."

Andrew ran lightly up the hill toward the castle. The moon was still shining, and there was enough light for him to see the woman standing in the path ahead of him. He dodged behind a gorse bush and watched. She was talking to someone — perhaps to the woman who had chased them. Their voices were low and hard to understand so that Andrew could not hear what passed between them.

He dared not overtake them. The moon that provided enough light to keep him from blundering into them on the path would give him away if he crossed the bare ground between them and the castle door. He wondered if he could circle around the castle and approach the door from the south-west corner.

The three other sides of rock upon which the tower stood were steep and rough. Dare he risk clambering around there in the dark?

The decision was made for him when the two women turned and walked back toward the huts. They passed within a few feet of him, and he thought that they must surely hear his pounding heart. They would find out that he was gone when they reached the hut, but there was nothing that he could do about that now. He waited a minute longer and then ran swiftly toward the castle. Even from several yards off, he could see the key in the door, glowing strangely.

He put a hand on the key and, as he did so, from somewhere to the south, he heard a strange, blood-curdling yell — a prolonged and frightening sound. Then there was a moment of intense silence, broken at last by the thin cry of a child in one of the huts by the pond.

When Andrew heard the yell he was filled with an almost uncontrollable desire to turn the key in the lock. It was as if the key itself were turning, and he had to use all his strength not to let it. He knew right then that turning the key would offer escape, but he realized that it would be cowardly to escape alone. What of Ian and Elinor down in the hut? What about little Ollie in the castle?

So he pulled the key from the door, and that simple act took more courage than all the adventures and battles that were to follow.

He wanted to get back to Ian and Elinor, but he felt uneasy about Ollie. She had not been with the women on the path, so there was a chance that she was alone in the keep and that he could talk to her. He pushed against the door, wondering if he could get in without using the key. It resisted at first, but it was only one of the cows that was in the way. The beast moved, and Andrew was able to open the door. He ran up the stairs to the main room. Ollie was there alone, still wearing the strange sack-like clothes.

"Come on, Ollie," he said in an urgent whisper. Who knew who might be watching and listening in the shadows?

Ollie looked at him warily, still plaiting and twisting the reeds from the floor.

"Ollie, come here!"

She did not come.

He crossed the room and caught her by the wrist. As he did so, she sank her teeth into the back of his hand. He jerked away, and blood showed where her even, white teeth had broken his skin.

He grabbed her by the shoulder and thrust her roughly across the room.

"We're going to find the others," he said, pushing her ahead of him down the stairs.

Once outside, he thought about the key again. It occurred to him that it might be better to hide it here, near the door, rather than risk carrying it around with him. The old woman had asked about the key and might take it from him.

He looked around for somewhere to hide it. Perhaps because they had buried the bird in a rabbit hole, he thought that might be a good place for it. Quite close to the door he spotted a hole among the roots of a gorse bush and thrust the key down inside. As he did so he happened to glance at Ollie and caught a strange, cunning look in her eye.

"You forget about that key," he said. "And come along with me."

Now that they were outside the tower, Ollie seemed more tractable and followed him. But halfway down the path — almost at the place where the two women had been talking — Andrew was rooted to the spot by the same blood-curdling yells he had heard before, and Ollie bolted back up the path. Andrew grabbed her and pulled her along with him down to the last hut.

There was now a great commotion around the huts, and people came pouring out of them, shouting to each other. But all was quiet around the last hut. Andrew thrust aside the skin and pulled Ollie inside. The candle had been lit again, and Andrew could see Elinor and Ian standing together near the door while the two women talked.

"Andrew! You've found Ollie! But what's going on out there?" asked Elinor. "I can't make out anything these old witches say, and now there's all this yelling and screaming. What's happening?"

Just then Ollie surprised them by breaking loose from Andrew's grasp and running to the ugly woman.

"Mama! Mama!" she said.

"There, there, ma wee bairn!" said the woman, cradling Ollie in her arms and rocking her gently back and forth.

"This is no time to croon over a bairn," said the older woman. "We have to decide what to do with these three and find the other one."

"The other one is Ollie. She's the fourth one," said Ian, pointing to Ollie.

"Nonsense!" said the old woman sharply. "That is Mae, the daughter of Muckle-mooth

Meg. She has been with us always. But it will not serve for us all to stand here and be slaughtered when the English attack. We must seek safety within the castle walls."

The woman picked up some skin blankets from a heap that lay on the floor and handed one to each of them. "Wrap yourselves in these. They will hide some of your strange garments, and you will need their warmth before the night is over."

Rather reluctantly — because they smelled — the children accepted the fur robes.

"Come!" said the woman, and they followed her out into the night. The moon had gone behind a cloud, but even without its light they knew that a great crowd was hurrying toward the castle.

3

The old woman led them to the main room
of the keep, which was now crowded with
women and children. Many of them had laid
blankets of coarse wool or skin on the floor
and were preparing to sleep. Others were
huddled near the fire, talking in low voices.
They paid little heed to the three strange children, and the woman motioned them to follow
her over to a corner.

Their corner was unlit, and cold air crept
in from the narrow window above. The stone
floor and stone walls were cold and damp,
and Elinor shivered in her thin summer

clothes. The old woman and the one called Muckle-mooth Meg were both with them, and Ollie — or Mae — was with them, too. She was careful never to leave hold of her mother's skirt.

"It makes me uneasy that they should turn up tonight, at the time when we are having trouble with the English," said Meg. "Does there not seem something strange about this attack — so much skirlin' and yellin'? Is it not more like these English to creep up and murder us in our sleep?"

"I, too, have been wondering about the way things are tonight," said the old woman. "Stay here with these children. I will be back."

And she disappeared into the shadows.

"Are you hungry?" Muckle-mooth Meg asked the children.

They nodded, more because they thought they might offend her if they refused food than because they felt real hunger.

"Get them meat," she told Mae.

The little girl wormed her way over to the fire and returned with a lump of meat, oozing juice and fat. It was torn into pieces, and each child was given a hunk. It was all Elinor could do to chew and swallow the meat, but she noticed that Mae was eating it with great enjoyment. It was the way Mae ate, more than anything, that convinced Elinor that the change in Ollie went beyond the change in her clothes. This child might look exactly like Ollie, but Ollie would never have tackled a piece of meat like that.

"What is the name of the old woman?" Andrew asked Meg.

"She is Anna, the seventh child of a seventh child, and she has the second sight. She told us of your coming and says you may spell the end of an age. Me, I do not know about these things, yet I do wonder where you have come from with your strange looks and clothes."

It was hard to understand what Meg said, for she slurred her words and the vowels were very broad. But as she talked, they gathered that the men had all gone from the castle and the village to raid the English cattle. The King — James of the Fiery Face, she called him — was going into battle and needed supplies for his soldiers. The Laird of Smailholm Tower had been asked to provide meat. Rather than kill his own cattle for the King, he had ridden off to steal what he needed from the English. All the men and older boys had gone on the raid, but Meg was afraid that something was amiss, for the

English were closing in on them, and their men had not returned.

While Muckle-mooth Meg was talking Mae crawled onto her lap, and now Meg began to sing softly to her. It was a sad, plaintive song, and as Andrew listened to it he tried to convince himself that it was all a dream. But the rich smell of roasting meat and the smoke itching in his throat and the pain in his hand where Mae had bitten him and the cold stone wall at his back were all too clear for the sensations of a dream. And the look of fear and perplexity in Elinor's and Ian's eyes was real, too.

Then he saw the old woman, Anna, threading her way across the room. She pointed a crooked finger toward him and said, "Come!"

He followed Anna up the winding stairs, and they entered the upper room. The floor was solid beneath their feet. He looked around with interest and, even by the meager light of Anna's candle, he could see that this upper room was better furnished than the room below. In one corner there were quite elaborate tapestries on the wall, and on a small table was a wooden cross.

Anna set the candle in a niche in the wall and opened a chest below it. She selected a few garments — trousers, a tunic, leather sock-like boots, and long thongs — and handed them to Andrew.

Andrew supposed she meant him to dress in these odd clothes, for she withdrew. They were made of leather but were well-worn and supple. They were also big, so that he was able to pull them on over his own jeans and T-shirt. Even the boots pulled on easily over his sneakers, but they were too long and slipped back down his leg. Then, prompted by some half-remembered picture in a history book, he took a thong of leather and criss-crossed it around his leg. It kept the boot firmly in place. He tied the other boot.

The clothes were comfortable and, feeling medieval and gallant, he took one or two prancing steps out into the middle of the room and executed a flourishing bow. He was mortified to find that Anna was standing in the doorway watching him. Even with everything so incomprehensible and strange, his feeling of embarrassment was completely real. He was still Andrew Elliot, who hated to be caught making a fool of himself!

"You will do," said Anna.

"Do for what?" asked Andrew.

"You are to take a warning to our men that the English are here. They have driven us into the castle with their skirlin' and noise, and now they have crept into our own houses by the lake and are lying in wait for our men to come home. We cannot fight them, but we cannot sit back and do nothing while they lay a trap for our men."

"What am I supposed to do?" asked Andrew, running his fingers through his untidy, brown hair.

"You must creep out and find our Laird Hepburn and warn him of the danger. You must go carefully, for we do not know that all the English are concealed in the huts. More may be waiting in the woods."

"But how can I?" protested Andrew. "I don't know the country, and I don't know your Laird. And he wouldn't know me. He wouldn't trust my message."

Andrew was vastly relieved that he had such good and valid arguments as to why he shouldn't go. He wouldn't have wanted the old woman to think him afraid.

"You will carry this dirk that belonged to the Laird, himself. He will then know that you come with a message from me." Anna handed him a short sword with a skillfully worked handle of silver. The blade was keen and glittered as she handed it to him.

"Wear it in your belt and it will offer both protection and the goodwill of the Laird."

"But I don't know where to go," said Andrew.

"The child, Mae, will lead you to the Beef-tub. It is a hollow in the hills where our men often take refuge when they are pressed, and they could be there now. Mae has been there with her grandfather, but it is too far for her to go alone."

The plan seemed more foolish than ever to Andrew. To send with him as a guide, the small child — Ollie or Mae, whichever she was — who did not like or trust him.

"She'll be more of a nuisance than a help," he said. "I'd do better going alone."

"We must hurry," said Anna, ignoring him.

"But how do you know you can trust me?" asked Andrew.

"The others — Elinor and Ian — are staying here." She spoke their names carefully, and he knew that it was a threat.

They went back downstairs, and Andrew saw from Elinor's and Ian's frightened look that they knew he was going to leave them. Meg, it seemed, was reluctant to let little Mae go with him, and she and Anna began to argue. Under the cover of their argument Andrew whispered, "If anything goes wrong, then you must use the key — but not unless you really have to."

"Where is it?" asked Elinor.

"It's hidden — in a rabbit hole near the door."

He had no time to say more because Anna, holding Mae by the hand, was beckoning him to follow. They climbed the stairs. Anna was talking to him, but Andrew was still thinking about the key and his feeling that it was somehow the answer to leaving this place, so he missed what she was saying. It came as a shock when she indicated that she wanted him to climb out of the narrow window. They were almost thirty feet from the ground and, if he fell, he would roll another thirty feet down the rocky cliff. There was a rope tied to a ring, and she clearly meant him to lower himself down on that.

He thought back to the gym at school and its dangling ropes and how he could only just make it to the top while some other boys climbed with ease. Climbing ropes wasn't his thing.

"Couldn't we use the door?" he asked. "They'll see us, dangling against the wall."

"We're on the north side, away from the houses. They will be watching the door. There is a chance you can make it this way if you hurry."

"What about her?" Andrew asked, nodding toward Mae.

"She has gone down the rope before. She is not afraid."

The old woman's voice was flat and expressionless so that Andrew could not tell if she meant to imply that he was afraid, or if she was merely stating that the girl could do it. At any rate, it was hard to delay longer, so he crawled backward across the window ledge and dropped his legs over the side. He hung awkwardly, trying to twist his feet around the rope. At least the soft leather of the boots gave good traction. Wriggling back, in an awkward fashion, he found himself wedged in the narrow window aperture. He couldn't make it. His shoulders wouldn't go through. But then he realized that he couldn't pull himself back up, either, and he didn't think the old woman would help him.

"You must waste no time," Anna said anxiously. "You must get out of the sight of the English before the dawn breaks across the sky."

Andrew eased his shoulders through and, with his full weight now on the rope, he went slithering down about ten feet, burning his hands before he managed to tighten the grip of his feet and brake the descent. He hung, swinging and bumping the wall, daring himself to continue.

Somewhere below he heard a twig snap and had the sudden fear that the English were covering this side of the castle. They might be watching him, hanging there, so vulnerable. Was someone down there at this moment fitting an arrow into his bow? It would come hissing through the air and land quivering in his spine. The thought froze him to the rope, and he waited for the bite of the arrow in his back.

He looked up and could see that the girl, Mae, was wriggling out of the window. He would have to slide down to get out of her way. His legs were trembling so much that he could hardly move, but somehow he inched himself down to the ground.

The girl landed beside him and began to scramble down the steep cliff. Twice, in the darkness, they dislodged stones which bounced and rattled down the hillside. If anyone was awake they must surely be alert by now, but there was no sound of pursuit.

The rough ground they were crossing, with its rocks and gorse bushes, offered good cover, but Andrew could see a lightening of the sky in the east. The sun would soon rise, and they must reach the woods before then.

The girl moved swiftly and confidently toward the trees and reminded Andrew of a small, alert animal. She covered the ground noiselessly and seemed to raise her head to sniff the air, constantly on the watch. Once or twice she stopped and motioned to him to wait. What she heard, Andrew did not know.

They reached the shadow of the wood and skirted along the edge of it until she beckoned him to follow her down an ill-defined path.

Andrew had no idea what direction they were taking. Under the trees he could no longer see the eastern sky, but the darkness was giving way to gray light. Mae was no longer quite so cautious, although she still walked quietly, and Andrew guessed that she was less afraid of the English now. But it was apparent that she still distrusted him. She greeted his questions with a blank hostile stare.

Quite suddenly they were on the edge of a river, too wide to cross.

"What do we do now?" Andrew asked.

Again Mae did not answer, but she changed direction, following the bank. Around the next bend Andrew saw a bridge. It spanned the river in a great symmetrical arch — a Roman bridge that had outlasted an empire. On their side of the bridge, next to the water, was a small meadow sprinkled with yellow buttercups and red campion. The sun was glancing through the trees, and the fresh greenness all around made the very air seem green.

"Let's rest here," said Andrew, and Mae seemed willing.

The glass glistened with dew, and a thin mist hung over the river. They walked through the meadow of wet flowers and disturbed a doe and fawn that had been drinking by the water's edge. The animals bounded back into the woods, and Andrew thought their graceful movement the most beautiful thing he had ever seen.

They went down to drink from the river, too. Unknown to them, other eyes had been watching the deer. Crouched in the brush, with narrowed yellow eyes, was a lean gray wolf. Cheated of the fawn for breakfast, it watched the small girl as she cupped her hands and drank from the river. It slithered forward, belly against the grass, and made no noise to betray its intent.

Andrew looked around, hoping for another glimpse of the fawn, and what he saw was the lithe gray form of the wolf creeping toward Mae. Instinctively, he grasped the dirk in his belt and drew it from its sheath. With a shout he jumped toward the wolf, hoping to drive it away. But the wolf was hungry and not about to be cheated a second time from its breakfast. It sprang, and Andrew raised the knife.

Andrew's actions in the fight that followed were instinctive rather than planned. The wolf sprang, and Andrew, defending himself with upraised arms, caught the angry beast across the throat with his knife. He was aware of the long, yellow teeth and the heavy smell of its fur. He was aware that there was blood on his hand but could not be sure where the blood came from. In a fury that came from fear rather than hate, he stabbed at the animal several times. Its front paws pushed against his chest, and he lost his footing and slipped so that he and the wolf rolled over onto the ground. But the wolf had been badly wounded, and its blood was matting its gray fur and staining the grass deep red. It twitched and whined, but Andrew had lost his fury and did not know how to finish off the fight that he had started. He would just have to leave it by the river while its life blood drained away.

"It was a good fight," said Mae, her eyes shining. "Do you mean to take the skin?"

"No," said Andrew.

"Is that not your first wolf? You cannot just leave it here to die."

"Come on," he said roughly. He was angry and upset by the fight. "We must find your grandfather."

Andrew would have liked to rest, but he could not stay there by the dying wolf and still did not have it in him to kill it.

Andrew and Mae climbed up a bank to the bridge and walked across it. It was fully light, but if the English were anywhere near, they would have heard them by the river anyway, so they took no precautions.

They continued to walk for a long time, following the road boldly, not bothering to hide. In fact, Andrew had forgotten about the English. All he could think about now was the wolf. Its evil eyes and yellow fangs did not trouble him, only the thought of it as it lay now, dying by the river. He wished he had been brave enough to kill it, to shorten its suffering, but when the fear had gone out of him, so had his courage.

The wolf had changed things between him and Mae, too. By killing it, he had saved her life — she knew that — and all her former distrust vanished. Also, she was getting tired and seemed less sure of where they were going.

The woods were behind them now, and they were climbing steadily into the hills. It was open country with a scattering of hawthorn and scrubby oak trees. They were still on the road and met not a soul.

Mae began to grumble. She was hungry and wanted Andrew to provide food. He gathered that she wanted him to catch a rabbit or a hare and cook it for them, but he had no idea how she expected him to do it. He wondered if Anna, also, had expected him to be able to provide food on the way, or if the journey was short enough that they could reach the Beef-tub without food.

The day had clouded over, but Andrew judged that it must be about noon. He was hungry, too, and very tired. Once or twice they stopped and rested, and he tried to question Mae about where they were going and when they would get there, but she seemed unable to explain.

"I will show you," was all she would say.

He talked to her of Ollie and London and Great Aunt Grace, but this brought no response at all. She was not puzzled by this talk, just completely disinterested. What he was saying was outside her comprehension.

"When will we eat?" she asked again.

"When we get there. You should know how long that will be."

She shook her head.

The hills around them were bare and smooth, old hills worn down by eons of passing time. And they were still being molded by the little streams that ran down their smooth flanks, cutting out miniature canyons. They stopped where one of these streams crossed the road, making pools of smooth brown mud, and Mae looked about with sharp interested eyes.

"This is the one," she said. "You must follow this stream back into the hills."

It looked no different from other streams they had crossed, and Andrew was reluctant to leave the road and climb straight up the hill. At least following the road gave the illusion that they were heading somewhere. Following the course of a tiny stream up the hillside seemed foolish.

Andrew was even more uncertain when Mae said she was too tired to go any further. She began to whine and cry and sounded so much like Ollie that he offered her a piggyback ride. But away from the road the ground was too rough and uneven, and Andrew only managed to walk a hundred yards or so before he had to put her down.

"I'll wait here," she said. "Go over the hill and bring my grandfather."

Andrew left Mae idly chasing minnows in the stream. Absorbed in her play, she again looked so like Ollie that Andrew was reassured and set off up the hillside alone.

The first part of the way he was hampered by bracken and heather, but further up the slope there was only short turf sprinkled with tiny flowers. Once he rested on a patch of purple thyme and looked back down on the way he had come. He could see no sign of Mae. She must be hidden by the bank of the stream or crouched down in the bracken.

He climbed on upward. The sun broke through the clouds, and he felt hot and sweaty in his tunic and leather boots. But he aimed at reaching a large outcrop of rock before he rested again.

Out on the hills, and with Mae far behind, the whole adventure seemed impossible. It was only his odd clothes and the dirk in his belt that reminded him that he was not just hiking through the Cheviot Hills. He was so busy thinking about what had happened that he was unprepared for what took place next.

He was almost at the rock when he heard a blood-curdling yell and two figures jumped from behind the rock and dragged him to the ground. Someone was kneeling on his back, pressing his face against the turf.

"Kill him and be done with him, I say," said one.

"Let's take him to the Chief," said the other.

"Finish him off, now! We want no spies around here!"

4

Andrew lay on the ground, unable to make sense of the argument that was going on above him. The one who wanted to take him to the Chief must have prevailed, because he was suddenly jerked to his feet and a scarf of some kind was bound over his eyes. In his tired and hungry state he had been finding the climb difficult before, but now, blindfolded and forced to go at a much faster pace, he stumbled and fell many times. Then he felt a change in the slope of the ground, and he seemed to be going downhill. The sun still shone on his left side so he did not think that they had turned around. He must be going down the other side of the hill.

Then he became aware of other voices and sounds close to him, and the scarf was pulled roughly from his eyes. He stood there, perplexed by the sudden light, and closed his eyes, not only against the light but also to shut out the scene before him.

He opened his eyes again and looked cautiously around. He was in the midst of a group of disheveled and uncouth men. They were dressed in tunics and cloaks, and all carried sticks or knives.

"What are you doing in these hills?"

The man who addressed this question to Andrew stood a little apart from the others. His bushy red hair and wild beard and heavy eyebrows made Andrew feel that he was facing a lion rather than a man.

"I am looking for Laird Hepburn," he said, feeling sure that this must be the Laird himself.

"What is your business with Red Hepburn?" the man asked.

"I have a message from Anna at Smailholm."

"I am Hepburn," said the red-haired man. "But how can you prove that you do, indeed, come from Smailholm and that you are not an English spy. You do not talk like one from these parts."

"Anna gave me this to give to you," said Andrew, pulling the dirk from his belt.

"Or you stole it," said the Laird. "How did you find your way here?"

"Your granddaughter, Mae, showed me the way."

"He was alone," broke in one of the men. "He lies! Kill him!"

"No! We must first find out the truth about the child. Where is she now?" asked the Laird. It seemed that with the mention of the child his expression had softened a little.

"She is waiting back down by the road. She was too tired to climb the hill."

"Go fetch your lass, Maxwell," the Laird said to one of the men who had captured Andrew. Then he turned back to Andrew and said, "My men will give you food, and then you can tell me more of who you are and why you have come. But if anything is amiss with the child, you will die by my sword."

Andrew looked at the long, broad, gleaming blade and prayed that little Mae had not wandered into any danger while he had been gone — both for her sake and his.

The men talked together, leaving Andrew time to look at his surroundings. They were in a saucer-shaped depression encircled by a ring of hills. They had entered at the lowest point on the rim. The entire bowl seemed to be full of men and cattle, and it made a good place of concealment. Sentries, posted on the hilltop, could keep track of their enemies.

One of the men brought Andrew a bowl of savory mutton stew, and since he was given no fork he picked up the pieces of meat with his fingers and then drank the gravy. The Laird went over to the pot and stabbed at the stew with a small dirk and then came over and joined Andrew.

"What is this message you bring from Smailholm? I have never seen you around here, have I? Where are you from?"

Andrew chose not to answer the last question but instead explained again that Anna had sent him.

"All the women and children ran for the castle when they heard the English coming," he said. "And now the English have crept into the houses by the lake and are waiting to take you by surprise when you return home."

"They would not dare do that," said Red Hepburn.

A smaller man with a swarthy but clean shaven complexion had joined them and had listened to what had been said.

"You do not think they would dare, do you, Douglas?" Hepburn asked him.

"The English could have reached Smailholm by now, for they were not hampered by these stupid cattle," Douglas answered. "Remember that it was because they were so close on our heels that we chose to hide here in the Beef-tub instead of making straight for the Tower. But surely they would not dare to fight us on our own land."

"This may be more than just a raiding party," said the Laird. "They may have wind of King James bringing his army south to retake Roxburgh Castle, and the English may be moving men north."

"So what this lad says could be true," said Douglas.

"And forewarned is forearmed," broke in Red Hepburn. "The success of their brazen plan depended on surprise, but now the surprise will be on them!"

" 'Twill be hard to surprise them when we have twenty of their cows lowing behind us," Douglas pointed out.

"We'll go round by Kelso and deliver the cattle to the King, and then, with a few of his men to help us, we'll make short work of the English at Smailholm. Let us march tonight and surprise them at dawn."

"The men will be glad enough not to spend another night on this windswept hilltop."

"Here is the little maid," said the Laird, looking up toward the rim of the hill. Turning to Andrew he said, "In that, at least, you spoke the truth."

Mae was riding on the shoulders of one of the men who had found Andrew, and he swung her to the ground.

"Grandfather! Grandfather!" she said, running up to the fierce Red Laird and throwing her arms around his legs. "You must not kill Andrew! He is no spy. He killed a wolf to save me, and he brings word from the Wise Woman, Grandfather."

"He killed a wolf, eh?"

"It was the biggest wolf I have ever seen, and he did not even take the skin. He said we must be on the road to warn you of the danger at Smailholm."

"Is this true?" asked the Laird. "Then surely you have earned the right to carry my dirk. It is yours."

An hour later they were ready to leave the concealment of the Beef-tub. Scouts made sure that no one was in sight when the cattle were driven over the edge of the rim. From there, men and cattle scattered and made their separate ways down the hillside to meet farther along the road. No one paid any attention to Andrew, and he felt rather lost as he followed along. He would even have sought out little Mae's company, but she was riding on the shoulders of one of the men and was half asleep besides.

It was a long walk, and the pace was slow because of the cattle. What talk there was, was lost to Andrew because he was too tired to take it in.

The rounded hills all seemed alike to him, but when they turned up a valley and followed the course of a tumbling stream through a wooded glen, Andrew was sure he had not been there before. The men were having trouble with the cattle, and Andrew found himself beside Maxwell, who was carrying Mae.

"This is not the way we came this morning," Andrew said.

"You came through the wood this morning. We are heading for Kelso now. We are going to give the cattle to the King. He has his army near Kelso."

"Will there be a fight tomorrow?" asked Andrew.

"There will, but we are going to leave you and the lass with the monks in Kelso. They will send you back to Smailholm tomorrow."

"Will the people in the tower be safe?"

asked Andrew, worrying about Elinor and Ian.

"The walls of Smailholm Keep are strong," answered Maxwell. "It is those outside the walls that will suffer."

Farther on, Andrew became aware that the dirt road under his feet had been replaced by cobblestones, and soon they were standing in front of huge gates. Maxwell rang a bell by the gate, and Andrew heard the slow, shuffling footsteps of someone coming to answer it. The gate swung open, and they were admitted by an elderly man in a brown monk's habit. Maxwell spoke briefly with the monk.

"Come, children," the monk said. "We will find you something to eat."

Andrew and Mae followed him through a small garden, rich with a tangle of sweet-smelling herbs, and then down a cloistered walk. From the Abbey itself they could hear the melodious rise and fall of voices chanting the evening vesper, and Andrew was moved by the peace and beauty around him. The monk led them to a big, low-ceilinged refectory and motioned them to be seated at one of the long tables.

They waited nervously and were glad when he returned with a plate of rolls and a pot of honey and a jug of milk. The two children ate ravenously, and when the plate was empty the monk led them to their sleeping quarters.

"You can share Cedric's room tonight," the monk told them. "It is small, but it backs onto the bread ovens so it is always warm. And Cedric can tell you anything you need to know."

The monk led them into a small room, little more than a cell, and left them to face the suspicious stare of a boy of about Andrew's age.

5

Meanwhile Elinor had not been finding waiting in Smailholm Tower easy.

When Andrew had come downstairs dressed in outlandish clothes and with some sort of sword in his belt, she thought that perhaps he, like Ollie, had become one of "them." Although he had whispered to her in Andrew's voice and shown some concern for her and Ian, she just did not think that her brother Andrew would set off on some secret mission in the night with a dagger at his side. It was ridiculous, and the adventure had lasted long enough.

She tried to ask, first Anna and then Meg,

where Andrew was going and when he would be back, but neither seemed disposed to answer her questions.

"Go to sleep, child," Meg told her. "It will pass the time of waiting."

"Where has Andrew gone?" Ian whispered to her.

"I think he went to warn someone that the English are outside," said Elinor.

"But we're English," said Ian.

"Hush," said Elinor, nervously. "Don't say that in here. I think the Scots and English are at war."

"Will there be a battle?" asked Ian.

"I don't know."

"I do hope we get to see a battle!"

"Not if I can help it," said Elinor. Then she realized that she didn't seem to have any control over anything that was happening — and there was Ian, accepting it all and hoping for a battle.

The fire had died down, and the room was dark. Most people had settled down to sleep, and Elinor could hear an occasional grunt or snore from old Anna, who lay near them, and occasional stirrings in other parts of the room. But there was no hope of sleep for Elinor. For one thing she had slept quite recently, and for another she was much too worried.

Lying in the darkness, she wondered what had happened to them and how they had penetrated the fabric of time and reached the lives of these distant people. But most of all she wondered how she could get back to the safe predictability of her own time. Perhaps the answer lay in the key. Andrew had whispered something to her about it.

She remembered Ian commenting on the luminous quality of the key that morning and became more and more certain that all she needed to do was turn the key in the lock and they would be safe — safe in their own time.

"Ian," she whispered. "Ian, come on!"

Ian had been lying awake in the darkness and sat up at once. She gripped his arm and pulled him over to the corner where the stairway led down through the wall. They felt their way down. She almost turned back when she heard the noisy breathing and shuffling of the cattle in the bottom room, but the idea of the key hidden outside the door was strong enough to overcome her fear of the cows.

"Come on," she said to Ian again. "Help me with the door."

Together they slid back the heavy bolt and

opened the door just wide enough to wriggle through. They pulled the door closed behind them and stood together in the encompassing darkness. The first dawn was streaking the eastern sky, and the small huts by the lake crouched silent and still.

"We must look for the key," said Elinor.

"But Andrew said not to use it unless we were in danger."

"Don't you want to get home?" she asked Ian.

"But what about Andrew and Ollie?"

"When we get there, they will be there too — where else could they be?"

"Here," said Ian. "I think we should wait for them."

His lower lip was trembling, and Elinor wondered what would happen if he began to cry. Ian cried rarely, but when he did it was no half-measure.

"We've got to find the key first, anyway," said Elinor. "Help me look for it. Andrew said he put it in a rabbit hole."

What Ian had said about Andrew and Ollie being left behind might be true, and Elinor didn't want to think about it. All she wanted was to get back to a world she could cope with. There wasn't enough light to search by. She only found two burrows at the base of a gorse bush and groped very gingerly in the soft earth. She got prickles in her fingers but found no key. Ian didn't even try to help but just sat by the door and waited.

"Let's go back inside," he said.

He had scarcely spoken when an arrow landed quivering in the heavy wooden door beside him. A slight sound from down by the huts betrayed where the arrow had come from.

"Quick! Get inside," said Elinor, and together they pushed open the door.

"We'd better go back upstairs."

The upstairs room seemed safer now, and they crawled back to their own corner. They did not sleep. Elinor sat watching the slit of sky she could see through the narrow window. Gradually it changed from black to gray to blue.

A woman stirred up the fire, and there was the welcome smell of some sort of bread baking. As Elinor became accustomed to the meager light, she could see quite a number of children, most of whom stayed close to their mothers. One or two played together, but for the most part they were content to scuffle occasionally and then sit still.

Breakfast consisted of a piece of dark

bread and a drink of ale which neither Elinor nor Ian liked. Then everyone settled in groups again and sat and waited. Ian was becoming more restless and daring. He left Elinor's side and began to play with another small boy of about his own age. It surprised Elinor that they were accepted by the group without questions. She decided it must be Anna's acceptance of them that satisfied the others. Anna seemed to be a person of status.

It was the longest day that Elinor could remember. She worried about Andrew and Ollie, and she worried about herself, but mostly she was unnerved by the air of waiting and listening that pervaded the whole room. What were they expecting to happen?

Toward evening the fire was built up and a pot of stew was hung over it. There was a general drawing together around the hearth.

"I wonder if the boy warned them," someone said.

"That we must wait and see," said Anna. "But they will not return in the night through the woods with the cattle, so we will not know until dawn."

"Let us have some music."

A girl of about Elinor's age plucked on a harp and began to sing in a beautiful melodious voice. The firelight glowed on her dark, tangled hair and even features. She pulled at the strings with long, pale hands, and the music sent shivers down Elinor's back. The surroundings were so dreary and the people so uncouth that it enhanced the beauty of the song and somehow made the feelings of the people real to Elinor. These people were waiting in fear for husbands and fathers to return, and they shared the same feelings she had. All this came to her through the music and the song, although she did not understand a word of it.

When the last notes faded away, there was silence and then someone asked Anna to tell a story.

Anna told stories of battles and treachery of long ago, and although Elinor could not follow much of it, she felt part of the listening circle in the firelight.

Then it was time to sleep again, and the people separated into family groups. Elinor and Ian went back to their corner beside Anna and huddled in their blankets. Elinor wished, not for the first time that day, that she had a hairbrush. She was becoming as untidy as all these people around her.

"Tell me about Mae," she asked Anna. She hoped that Anna, having been in the mood for telling stories, would tell her something about Mae that might shed some light on the mystery of the interchange between Ollie and Mae.

To her surprise, old Anna chuckled. "Mae is the child of Muckle-mooth Meg. Yes, there is a story there, and I see no harm in telling you.

"Seven years ago the Maxwells sent a big raiding party up this way — that happens all the time, of course — a thieving lot, these Maxwells are. Robert Maxwell, always a mite bolder than the rest, came right to our very door and stole one of our cows. It was his great mistake to choose one that was more stubborn than all the rest and, although the man has cunning and guile, he did not get away with it. He was caught and brought before the Laird, Red Hepburn.

"The penalty for stealing another man's sheep or cow is hanging. But Laird Hepburn saw that this was a fine, upstanding man, and it seemed a pity that he should hang, for Hepburn had a daughter that was in need of a husband. His oldest daughter, Meg, was a kindly girl, but — well, you have seen her — she had never found a suitor.

"So the Laird called Maxwell before him and said that his life would be spared if he would swear loyalty to the Hepburns and wed his eldest daughter. Maxwell agreed to the deal.

"However, when Muckle-mooth Meg was called out, the bridegroom took one look at the poor, plain girl and said, 'I'd rather hang!'

"So the gallows were erected and a crowd gathered and Maxwell was led out to his death. He took one look at the gallows and another look at the lass, and now she did not look quite so bad, so he said, 'I'll take the girl!'

"It was a good choice he made. Meg has been a fine wife and bore him a little daughter, Mae, whom they both love dearly. A clever and bonny child, she is. And Maxwell has been loyal to his oath."

The story didn't cast any light on Ollie and Mae, but somehow Elinor was comforted to know that they loved Mae and that she was a happy child.

That night, in spite of the strangeness of their surroundings and the cold floor, both Elinor and Ian slept, tired out by the long day of waiting.

Elinor was wakened by the sound of a scream that froze the very blood in her veins.

"What is it? What is it?" asked Ian. His

eyes were wide with terror. "What's happening, Elinor?"

The scream died away, leaving an instant of silence, and then there was an explosion of yelling and shouting. The battle that Ian had hoped for was being fought down among the huts by the lake. Those inside the castle had no part in it, and once again all they could do was wait.

It wasn't long before there was a great hammering at the door and it was flung open to admit the victorious Scots.

Although those inside had missed the battle, they were not spared the bloody aftermath. It had only been a short skirmish because the English had been unprepared for the speed and direction of the attack and were quickly routed. But the Scots did not gain their victory unscathed, and the sick and bleeding were carried up to the keep. One man — quite young he looked — had a fearful gash in his thigh, and another had an arrow in his side. He screamed with pain when old Anna cut it out.

Elinor wished that she could help. There should have been drugs to numb the pain, and the young man should have had stitches in his leg, not a plaster of mud and a bandage of rags. But there was nothing she could do

— she really didn't know any more than Anna did. She could tell these people about X-rays and blood transfusions and the miraculous things that doctors could do, but she couldn't make any of these things happen.

Ian was at her side, tugging at her sleeve.

"Where are Andrew and Ollie?" he asked. "They haven't come back."

Andrew and Ollie! How could she have forgotten them! She ran up to Anna, who was still trying to stem the flow of blood from the arrow wound in the man's side.

"Where is Andrew?" she asked. "Is he all right?"

Anna turned and spoke to a tall, dark-haired man behind her.

"Maxwell, did your daughter and a lad bring a warning to the Laird?"

"Aye, they did. We nearly ran a dagger through the boy before he spilled his story. He and the lass are safe at Kelso Abbey. They should be here by noontime."

"They are all right," Anna said to Elinor. "Now, you keep yourselves hidden over in the corner until I have time to think over the meaning of your coming. Stay away from the men."

Elinor and Ian were not anxious to draw

attention to themselves, so they went back to their corner and waited.

They waited all day, and Andrew and Ollie did not come. All around them was noise and excitement and confusion, but they had no part in it. Then they saw Meg sitting by the fire, her loom idle. She, too, was waiting for a child to come home.

6

The monk who showed Andrew and Mae to the small room where they were to sleep had left them saying that the boy, Cedric, would tell them anything they needed to know. But Cedric had more questions than answers.

"Who are you, and where are you from?" he asked.

"I am Andrew Elliot from Smailholm," Andrew answered cautiously.

"You talk as if you were foreign to these parts," said the boy.

"In a way I am," answered Andrew, knowing there was no way in which he could tell the whole story. "This is Mae, the granddaughter of the Laird of Smailholm, and we had to take a warning to him."

"Warning of what?" Cedric asked suspiciously.

So Andrew described his adventures of the day, and Cedric listened with great interest, especially when Mae broke in and told about the fight with the wolf.

"You killed it with your own dirk?" he asked. Andrew showed Cedric the knife, and he fingered the blade with reverence.

"What wouldn't I give for that," he whispered.

"You don't have a knife?" asked Andrew.

"Here? In the Abbey? No, we have no need of weapons here, they say. But some day I will be a soldier. They cannot make me be a monk."

"What are you doing here?"

"I used to travel with my father. He was a peddler and went from town to town. I can barely remember those days. He was set upon and killed, and one of the monks found me. They have been kind to me, but I get a great longing to see the world outside these walls."

The boy knew much of what was going on outside the walls. The monastery was a great place for rumors and gossip, and Cedric heard all of it. He told Andrew that King James II was marching south from Edinburgh and was planning to take Roxburgh Castle from the English. It had been in English hands too long, and now that they were fighting among themselves about whether the House of Lancaster or the House of York should rule, it was a good time to force them out of one of Scotland's castles. More than anything, the boy wanted to have a share in retaking the castle.

As he listened, Andrew felt sure that he had enough clues at last to tell him the date — James II was King of Scotland and the houses of Lancaster and York were fighting in England — but he had not paid enough attention to his history books. He wasn't even sure of the century, let alone the year.

Cedric was still talking enthusiastically about James' chances of driving the English out of Roxburgh Castle. "It will be a great battle," he said. "The King has a cannon that will blow the walls apart and send all the Englishmen back over the border in a cloud of smoke."

"It will be a year that will go down in history," said Andrew.

"Yes," said Cedric. "They will long remember 1460 as the year we drove the English out of Roxburgh Castle."

"Fourteen-sixty!" echoed Andrew, excited to have found out so much without having to ask a direct question.

"Red Hepburn's men will be in the thick of the battle. Will you be there?" asked Cedric.

"I don't know," said Andrew. "What's to stop you from joining them?"

"In these clothes?" said the boy. "And what would I fight with? This battle will be more than throwing a few rocks."

It was too dark for Andrew to make out what the boy was wearing, but he touched the knife in his belt and thought that Cedric would surely like it better than he did. Was it cowardly to be afraid to kill?

Then Andrew made himself comfortable in a heap of straw. As he was drifting off to sleep, he wondered how Ian and Elinor had spent the day. He felt a little guilty that he had not thought about them more because he had a sudden suspicion that they had probably been thinking about him, especially if they had spent the whole day waiting inside Smailholm Tower.

The slow peal of a bell penetrated Andrew's dream, and he woke in a state of complete disbelief. Where was he? Straw tickled his neck, and he stretched his stiff limbs. What was he wearing?

Gradually he realized that sleep had not dispelled the unreality of yesterday. He was in a small room, and beside him was a chubby, untidy, fair-haired child who must surely be Ollie but who spoke in the broad dialect of some other time and only knew him as the boy who saved her from the fangs of a wolf.

He turned away from Ollie to find that he was in turn being scrutinized by the boy Cedric. There was now enough light in the small room for him to see that Cedric was a ginger-haired boy with freckles and friendly blue eyes. He was clad in a shapeless brown garment and wore sandals on his feet. He grinned at Andrew, and one of his front teeth was very crooked.

"I have to go and help in the bakehouse," said the boy. "Come with me, and you might get some hot bread."

However, before they even reached the bakehouse they were met by the monk who had looked after them the night before.

"Now that you are rested, you should be on your way," he said to Andrew and Mae. "It has been arranged that Cedric will go with you to show you how to reach Smailholm."

Cedric was only too pleased to accompany them. He looked on a day away from the

Abbey as a real holiday, and his high spirits were catching.

Outside the Abbey gates there were all sorts of merchants selling their wares, and although the children had no money they wandered around looking and listening. There was such a festive air that they did not want to leave. It was only when Cedric filched an apple from a barrel and a big man, brandishing a stick, chased the three of them down an alley to the river that they decided it was time to be on their way.

Cedric good-naturedly shared the apple with them. They walked along the riverbank through woods and bushes. Little Mae gathered wild flowers, and the boys skipped stones across the water. Cedric saw a crow's nest high in a tree and scrambled up but could not reach it. Andrew tried but didn't get as high as Cedric. They swung on branches and chased rabbits and threw stones. Their progress was slow.

Around noon Cedric produced some small, flat barley cakes from a deep pocket. They ate them hungrily and drank water from the river.

"I'm going to have a swim," said Andrew, looking at the inviting water of a clear, deep pool.

Cedric hung back, and Andrew knew from the way he looked at the water that this was something he would do better than Cedric. He stripped off his clothes, aware that Cedric was watching him curiously, and plunged into the river.

Cedric took off his brown robe and entered the water slowly. Andrew came over splashing and shouting, and Cedric soon overcame his caution and tried to imitate Andrew's swimming strokes. Mae paddled along the edge, floating the garlands of flowers she had been making.

When they began to feel cold they scrambled up the bank, and the sight of their bundled clothes gave Andrew a sudden idea.

"Cedric, why don't you take my trousers and tunic, and then you could go and fight your battle if you want to!"

The fact that they weren't even his clothes to give away did not occur to Andrew.

Cedric looked at him in amazement. Then his blue eyes sparkled and he grinned, showing his crooked tooth.

"You would let me?" he asked.

"Sure! Have the knife, too!"

The boys dressed in each other's clothes. Cedric was so excited that he paid little attention to the jeans and shirt that Andrew put on under the robe, though they must have seemed strange indeed. Cedric swaggered around, brandishing the dirk, and Andrew laughed. Was it only yesterday that he had felt the same way when he tried on these clothes? It seemed longer than that. Then Andrew clasped his hands in front of him and with mock piety shuffled along the path, and Cedric, in his turn, laughed.

But Mae was getting tired of their fooling. Her flowers were wilted, and she was hungry again.

"We'd better go," said Andrew. "Is it far?"

"It is quite a long way," answered Cedric. "Maybe if we take the path over the hill, we will find some berries for her to eat."

So they cut over the hill, and they did find blueberries — but scarcely enough to justify the extra miles they walked to find them.

"Yonder is the tower," said Cedric, and they could see Smailholm standing on its rock, etched against the evening sky. "You can find your way from here."

Then he asked, "Are you sure I can have the clothes and dirk? I would not want anyone to think I had taken them from you."

"Keep them," said Andrew. "But where will you go?"

"I plan to go to Roxburgh and help the King drive the English out of the castle."

The two boys parted, and Andrew hated to see Cedric go.

"I'm tired," said Mae.

Andrew hoisted her onto his back and carried her most of the rest of the way to the tower.

7

Andrew walked slowly toward the keep. He
had wasted so much time with Cedric that
now he was afraid of what he might find
there. Had the Scots driven off the English?
Were Elinor and Ian safe?

Smailholm Tower looked menacing against
the evening sky. The setting sun was behind
it, so the stone appeared solid and black and
the castle cast a long shadow. However, it
seemed that the families had moved back into
the little thatched huts by the lake because he
could see one or two children playing in the
doorways. Mae called out to them as she

passed by, but she continued up the path to the keep and Andrew followed her.

The big door stood wide open. Mae scrambled up the stairs, but Andrew hung back. From the room above he could hear a strange wailing cry that rose and fell like the wind in the pine forest. Anxiously he felt his way up the stairs, wondering what he would find. Almost before he entered the room, and certainly before his eyes had adjusted to the dim light, he heard Elinor call his name.

She came running over and hugged him.

"What on earth is that noise?" Andrew asked, ignoring Elinor's unusual greeting.

"It's Hannah, over there in the window seat. Her husband died. It was terrible — he had an arrow in his side, and Anna couldn't save him. Andrew, I want to go home."

"Home?" Andrew repeated the word as if it had no meaning to him.

"Yes, home! Back to our own time."

"I don't know that we can decide that," said Andrew slowly.

"But the key! You said that the key would take us back." Elinor pulled at his sleeve. "Please try the key. Where is it?"

"What have you been doing?" asked Andrew.

"What have I been doing?" echoed Elinor

78

shrilly. "I've been sitting around waiting for you to come back. I've done nothing but wait."

"But wasn't there a fight — when Hannah's husband . . ."

"I was in here, and the fight was going on outside," interrupted Elinor. "Not that I wanted to see the battle, but I thought you and Ollie might be out there. It was awful. And where is Ollie?"

"She's with her mother now. She came back with me."

"Her mother?"

"She's still Mae, you know."

"Don't you want to get away from here?" wailed Elinor.

"Does Ian?" Andrew asked.

Ian was wrestling on the reed-strewn floor with a small boy, and they were both dusty and disheveled.

"It hasn't been as bad for him. He plays around like he belongs."

Then Elinor noticed Andrew's cloak and asked, "What's that you're wearing?"

"A monk's robe," said Andrew.

"A monk's robe! Where have you been?"

"It belonged to a boy called Cedric. He wanted to fight in the battle to take Roxburgh Castle, so I lent him my clothes."

Elinor gave Andrew an incredulous look and asked, "How can you stand there and talk about Cedric and monk's robes and battles as if they were all real? I want to get away from all this."

While they had been talking, several men had come into the room, and Andrew noticed that Laird Hepburn was among them. It seemed that he had something of importance to say because a crowd had gathered around and there was much shouting and cheering.

"Couldn't we please try the key?" asked Elinor.

"Not without Mae," said Andrew. "I suppose she went upstairs. Come on and see if we can find her."

"Upstairs?" said Elinor. "We were told to stay here."

"Well, you wait and I'll go," said Andrew.

"No!" broke in Elinor. "I'm not letting you go off again. We'll all go."

She went over and pulled Ian away from his game, and they went upstairs with Andrew in the lead, their hands on the rough walls, feeling their way. The upper room was lit by candles, and from the doorway they could see that both Mae and her mother were there. Muckle-mouth Meg was in the corner of the room where the tapestries hung on the wall, kneeling on the floor before the wooden cross.

She must have heard them, for she turned around abruptly.

"There you are," she said to Andrew. "I was giving thanks to God that my man and bairn are safe. Mae tells me that you saved her from a wolf."

Andrew stepped into the room and was about to give a modest answer, but Elinor gave a snort of either surprise or disbelief behind him, so he didn't say anything. It wouldn't hurt for her to realize that he had been facing real danger out there while all she had to complain about was waiting.

"He fought with it," said Mae.

"I wish I'd been there," said Ian. "I'd have killed it, too!"

"What are you children doing here?" Meg asked. "Anna, who always talks in riddles, says you will mark the end of an age with the turn of a key. What does she mean?"

"We don't understand it, either," answered Andrew. "It just happened."

"Where did you come from?"

Before Andrew could try to answer, he was interrupted by a cry from the doorway.

"Will there be no peace in our time?"

The children spun around to see Anna

standing behind them, her witch-like features exaggerated by the light thrown up from the candle she held.

"Word has come that the King is going to make his long-awaited attack on Roxburgh Castle and drive the English out forever. Our men are going to join him in battle."

"When?" asked Meg.

"They are leaving now."

"My prayers of thanks have scarce risen to heaven before I need pray for their safe-keeping again."

"They need food and warm clothes as much as they need your prayers," said Anna. "Maxwell is shouting for you to bring him his cloak."

Back downstairs, the room was in tremendous confusion. The woman was still wailing on the window seat, but she had just become a fraction of the noise that was going on.

"Come, men, we must be ready if we are to fight beside our King at dawn. James of the Fiery Face will drive these English from our land forever with his great cannon."

This was greeted by a mighty cheer, and even Andrew and Ian joined in. As Andrew listened to the stirring sound of Red Hepburn's words, his thoughts turned to Cedric, who would also be fighting for his King.

Quite suddenly he wanted desperately to see Cedric again.

"I'm going with them," he said to Elinor.

"You are not," she said. "You're not going to leave me here waiting again."

"Well, you can't come," said Andrew. "It's just men."

"That's no argument," said Elinor. "I can do anything you can do."

"But this is the fourteen hundreds," argued Andrew. "Girls didn't fight in battles."

"How about Joan of Arc?" Elinor asked triumphantly.

"You're no Joan of Arc," said Andrew rudely. "Not in your jeans and that blanket."

"You don't look like a warrior either, in that dumb brown dressing-gown. Who ever heard of going to war in a dressing-gown!"

Elinor had touched on a problem, all right. Andrew found himself wishing that he had not given his clothes to Cedric. But then, of course, Cedric would not be among the King's soldiers if Andrew had not given him the clothes and dirk.

"They wouldn't let you go, anyway," said Elinor.

As it turned out, the Laird did not seem to care much who went along. He gave a rallying cry and, with much shouting and singing, the men surged through the door and down the hill. Andrew suspected that they had been drinking too much ale celebrating routing the English from their huts that morning and were now spoiling for another fight. The noise and confusion were so great that Andrew and Elinor were ignored, even though Elinor was shouting at him like a nagging wife. She half-wanted to go with him but felt that she couldn't drag Ian along, too, and she had too much conscience to leave him. How could Andrew act so recklessly?

"I'm going to look for the key," she warned him. "And I'm going to use it!"

"I just want to see Cedric again," said Andrew. "I won't fight in the battle."

"But who is Cedric?"

Andrew had no time to answer. The men were on their way. The Laird was mounted, and several dogs ran yapping behind him. There was no attempt at stealth or silence.

Before long, much of the enthusiasm went out of the men and, after stumbling and cursing for many miles (or so it seemed to Andrew), they reached a place by the river where they stopped to rest. It was now dark, and most of the men wrapped themselves in their cloaks and slept. Andrew, huddled in his monk's robe a little apart from the others, could not sleep.

He was regretting his impetuous decision to see the battle. It wasn't likely that he would find Cedric, and he now felt guilty that he had left Elinor and Ian and Ollie again. Besides, he didn't belong with this wild band of men. There were no boys of his age and the men ignored him, just as they had on the walk back from the Beef-tub.

At long last it began to get light. Andrew stayed apart from the group, afraid that his monk's habit might cause comment. Some of the men produced loaves of hard, dark bread and gnawed on them, but they did not share with each other or with Andrew. So all he had for breakfast was a drink from the river and some blackberries that were growing nearby.

Then the men gathered their few belongings together and moved on quietly, whether by design or because their exuberance was gone Andrew could not tell. The country was sparsely wooded, but they soon came out into a vast open area beside the river.

Then Andrew looked up and saw the castle. It was a huge, magnificent fortress with the River Tweed flowing in front of it and the Teviot behind. The barriers made by both nature and man — the rivers and the great impenetrable walls — showed why the castle was so hard to conquer. In the past, the only way to take it had been by siege or by guile, but now it was boasted that the Scots with their mighty cannon, the Lion, would blow the walls to bits.

All around was noise. Andrew found that he was not so out of place as he had feared. The Scottish army seemed to consist of disorganized bands of men, each under their own leader, without any apparent understanding of the overall plan. Andrew's main concern was not to be knocked down and trampled by the Scots. At this time he had no fear of the English, who seemed quite remote behind the walls of the fortress.

Then word reached Laird Hepburn's men that the King himself was coming. It may have been an attempt on James' part to bring unity to his men, or it may have been to assess his own strength, but he came riding around the field to greet the clans in person.

A cry went up, "The King! Long live the King!"

Andrew forgot about remaining inconspicuous and pushed forward to see.

The King was a lean young man, mounted on his horse with arrogant pride. When he came close and turned to speak to Laird Hepburn, Andrew saw that his face was disfigured by a terrible red birthmark — James of the Fiery Face. But it was the determined light in the King's eye — not the impression of the disfigurement — that stayed with Andrew. Here was a man looking for victory, no matter what the cost.

And it was to cost him his life.

Not so very much later in the day, King James sat mounted on his horse, a little behind and to the right of the great Lion, the hooped gun which would breach the castle walls and drive the English out of Scotland. He watched his soldiers load and prime it and then gave the signal to fire. Before the words were even spoken, the whole gun exploded in a tremendous burst of flame and smoke. A piece of flying metal found its mark and killed the King.

The battle was not over. Other guns were fired, and men swarmed across the river, risking the shower of arrows from the English archers, high on the castle walls.

Andrew, however, had lost his liking for the battle. The rumor of the King's death had traveled quickly, and the idea that the proud determined man whom he had just seen had been killed by his own clumsy gun was terrible. It hurt him to think about it — it was all so senseless.

Red Hepburn and his men had moved

ahead, and now Andrew lingered on the edge of the battle, wondering what he should do. Yet he was drawn forward, down to the river, on the fringe of a tide of movement.

He was now within range of the hail of arrows from the castle wall, and the noise and smoke were worse than ever. All day he had allowed himself to be drawn along by the crowd, but now, if he didn't want to be in the thick of the battle, he would have to think for himself.

Then, the roar of the battle — smoke and song — was severed from his mind and his whole concentration centered on one small area of grass and mud beside the river. Half supported by a willow bush, pierced in the side by a stray arrow, was a red-haired boy. His mouth, taut in a grimace of pain, showed his crooked front tooth.

"Cedric!" said Andrew, kneeling in the mud beside him. "Cedric! It's Andrew."

Cedric opened his eyes, and his breath came in short jerks.

"Can you help me?" he asked.

Andrew tried to help him back to drier ground, but Cedric sobbed with pain, so Andrew took off his brown monk's garb, spread it on the ground, and eased Cedric onto it.

"I saw the King," whispered Cedric. "And

did you see yon gun? We'll drive the English out. The King will fire his gun."

Andrew did not tell Cedric that the King was dead.

"It was a great battle," said Cedric.

And then he closed his eyes. For poor young Cedric the battle was over.

Andrew stumbled away. Afterward he had no memory of the walk back to Smailholm. How he found his way through the woods he did not know, but once again he reached the castle as dusk descended. Again the castle stood black against the evening sky, and Andrew ran toward it.

8

Andrew was scrambling up the last slope to the castle door when Mae appeared beside him.

"You went with my father to take Roxburgh Castle from the English," she said. "Did you see the battle?"

Andrew nodded his head.

"Did they take the castle? I saw it once, and the walls are strong and high. But the King has a great gun, and Anna says he will drive out the English."

"Where are Elinor and Ian?" Andrew asked.

But Mae was clearly not interested in

Elinor and Ian. Her mind was on Roxburgh Castle. "Did you fight in the battle?" she asked. Then she added, "But you did not have your dirk. Cedric was going to fight with it."

Andrew was surprised that Mae knew this. She did not seem to pay much attention to what was going on around her, but Andrew remembered that she was the one whom Anna had chosen to show him the way to the Beeftub. Perhaps she knew more than he gave her credit for.

"Where are Ian and Elinor?" he asked again, but again she did not answer.

They were standing beside the door, and Andrew knelt down and looked in the burrow where he had hidden the key. This time when Elinor wanted to go home he would be ready to go with her. The burrow was beside a gorse bush, and he knew exactly where to look. His fingers groped in the soft earth and finally closed on something hard and cold, but it was only a stone. The key was not there. He searched more thoroughly — still finding nothing. Then he felt a moment of panic. Elinor and Ian must have found the key and used it. They had left him behind.

He felt a surge of anger and then it subsided. He had been unfair. He had left them waiting and waiting and had not even tried to let them share the adventures. Well, he hadn't had such a great time either — except for the day with Cedric. But the battle first-hand had been awful. And there would be no more carefree days for Cedric.

What would happen to him now?

It was his turn to wait. He climbed the spiral stair, and the main room was empty. The fire was burning low and a pot was simmering beside it, but the corner where Elinor and Ian slept was bare. Even the skin blankets were gone.

Andrew went over and sat down by the fire, unsure of what he should do next. No wonder Elinor had complained. Waiting and feeling uncertain were much harder than doing.

He sat there for a long time and was finally joined by little Mae.

"They didn't take you with them," he said.

"I didn't want to go."

"When did they leave?" he asked.

"After Anna found that you had gone with the men to battle, she took them down to her hut. I think she is afraid because she does not understand what your coming means."

"You mean they are still here," said Andrew incredulously. "They are down in her hut?"

Mae nodded.

"Is Anna with them?" Andrew asked.

"I think she is in the upstairs room with my mother. They talk together because they are afraid."

"I'm going to find Elinor and Ian," said Andrew. "Are you coming?"

He didn't wait for her to answer but ran from the room and down the steep path to the last hut beside the lake. He pushed aside the skin door and stepped inside.

"Elinor! Ian!"

They were sitting together on the floor and jumped up when he came in.

"You're back!" said Elinor. "Are you all right?"

"Yes, and I've had enough. I'm ready to go home."

"I'm glad to hear you say that," said Elinor. "Do you have the key?"

Andrew shook his head. "I hoped you had it. I thought you had taken it and used it and left me here. I was really scared."

"We did look for it," said Elinor. "The first time Ian nearly got hit by an arrow, and the next time Anna caught us and she was very angry. That was when she brought us down here, and this is worse than the castle. It's so dark and it smells and I wish I had a hairbrush. I feel such a mess."

"A hairbrush?" said Andrew. "It's the key

that we need. Do you think Anna found the key?"

"I don't think so," said Ian. "I think Mae has it. And I think she might give it to you."

"To me?" asked Andrew.

"Yes," said Ian. "She likes you best because you killed the wolf. Tell us about it, Andrew."

"Not just now. We've got to get the key. Let's find Mae."

Mae was sitting outside the hut. Andrew wondered if she had been listening to them.

"Where's the key, Mae?" he asked her.

She didn't answer, but a look of cunning crossed her face so that Andrew felt sure she knew about it.

"What do you have in your pockets?" Andrew asked, turning to Elinor and Ian.

Elinor pulled out a crumpled tissue and a hairclip. Andrew glanced at Mae's tangled hair and turned his attention to Ian's pockets. He had more of interest — a pocket knife, a rather fuzzy toffee, and three marbles.

"I didn't know I had that," he said, popping the toffee in his mouth.

"Ian!" said Andrew. "That was probably the best thing we had. How could you eat it? I wanted something to trade for the key."

"I'm hungry," said Ian. "I'm always hungry here."

Andrew showed Mae the knife, but she was not interested. However, she did reach for one of the marbles.

"Not the green one!" said Ian.

"We'll give you the marbles for the key," said Andrew.

"That's my best one," said Ian, as Mae took the green marble and held it up to the light.

"Where is the key?" asked Andrew.

Mae started off up the path toward the castle, and they followed her, with Ian still grumbling about his marble. Elinor and Andrew were becoming frantic as they listened to Ian, but actually his fussing was having the right effect on Mae. She began to want the green marble as much as he did and was prepared to give up the shiny key to get it.

Close to the door she stopped and looked around and then ran to a big flat stone. She strained and tugged at the stone and finally lifted it. Under it lay the key, still with the same soft glow.

Andrew handed her Ian's marbles and took the key. From inside the keep he could hear the sound of running feet and the voices of Anna and Meg calling Mae's name.

"Help me with the door," Andrew shouted. Elinor came running to his side, and together they slammed the heavy door. Andrew thrust the key in the lock with shaking fingers.

"Quick, they're coming," said Elinor.

A rook, perched in one of the high, narrow windows, gave a harsh cry and flew straight down toward them, a great black shape with beating wings. Elinor held her arms up over her face to fend it off, and the key turned in Andrew's hand.

The harsh cry of the bird dissolved into silence and, for a moment, time stood still.

Then the children looked around them. A lark was suspended in the blue sky above, a lamb was bleating, the thatched huts were gone, and Aunt Grace's cottage stood solid and real, down by the road where it belonged.

"We're home! We're home!" said Elinor with a great sigh of relief.

"We're all safe," said Andrew. "I was so afraid that the key might not be the answer after all."

"Look at Ollie," said Ian.

They turned toward Ollie. There sat their chubby, blond little sister, but she was still wearing the homespun garment of another time. In her hands were three marbles, and her eyes met theirs with complete bafflement and distrust.

9

Andrew, Elinor, and Ian sat looking doubtfully at Ollie. They were none of them very clean — even Elinor — but Ollie was by far the worst. They could see the snarls and tangles in her hair. Her face and arms were gray with dirt. And, of course, her clothes were all wrong.

"I want Mama," said Ollie, speaking at last, and she spoke in the flat, broad voice of Mae. "I want Mama!"

"Hush, Ollie," said Elinor. "Mother went to France."

"Mae," she sniffed. "And I want to go home."

She looked up at the castle door and then reached for the key in Andrew's hand.

The key was solid and black now. Perhaps that was why Andrew allowed Ollie to take it. She opened the door and went inside, but the others did not follow. They sat on the big rock near the door, looking down on Aunt Grace's cottage. Aunt Grace had come out into the garden and was hanging tea-towels on the wash-line. They caught a glimpse of a car speeding along the narrow road, and then it was lost from sight between high hedges. A tractor chugged noisily in a field. Everything was as it should be.

Everything — except for poor Ollie-Mae.

A hoarse cry from inside the castle told them that she had reached the main room and found it empty. The benches, candles, cooking pot, and wall hangings were gone. And the people were gone, too.

She came stumbling out into the sunlight, looking very small and forlorn. She was so little — only five-going-on-six, and she was lost — not just in space, but in time.

"It was that way for us, too," said Elinor gently. "We were scared when we found we were in your time. We'll look after you."

Ollie looked at them without giving any indication that she heard or understood.

"What should we do?" asked Andrew.

"First we have to get her cleaned up," said Elinor. "We'll have to pretend she's Ollie until we get the real Ollie back."

"But where is Ollie?" asked Ian. "We don't know where she is."

"It will be quite easy to fool Aunt Grace," Elinor continued, ignoring Ian's question. It was too disturbing. "Aunt Grace hardly knew Ollie. As long as Mae doesn't talk much we can get away with it."

"Why don't we just tell Aunt Grace?" asked Ian.

Again Elinor and Andrew paid no attention to him.

"I think we have to go back and look for Ollie," said Andrew.

"I'm not going back there," shouted Elinor. "It was all right for you, rushing about killing wolves and fighting battles, but I sat in that room for three days."

Then she paused and spoke more quietly. "Three days. How come they aren't looking for us? How come Aunt Grace is down there hanging out her washing if we've been missing for three days?"

"I don't think it has been three days here," said Andrew. "In fact, I don't think it really happened. It was just an illusion."

"And is Mae an illusion?" asked Elinor.

"Well, that's harder to explain."

"You don't know what you're talking about," said Elinor crossly.

"You're right," said Andrew and shrugged. "And about going back. I'm not sure that we can. After all, Mae used the key just now and it didn't take her back."

"The key's not shiny anymore," said Ian. "It lost its magic."

How much easier to be seven years old and accept magic, thought Andrew.

"We have to clean her up," said Elinor firmly.

"And we don't want Aunt Grace to see her," said Andrew. "Maybe she'll go to town later on. I'll go down and see if she plans on going out."

"I'm going, too," said Ian. "I want to get my paddle-wheeler."

"To get your what?"

"My boat. Ollie always wanted to play with it, and I never let her. Maybe Mae would like it."

"O.K. Come along! But we're going to call her Ollie all the time. Forget Mae, and maybe she will, too."

So Elinor was left alone with Ollie-Mae. It was awful to feel so uncomfortable with the child. She could think of nothing to say, so they sat in silence. Elinor was greatly relieved when Ian came running back.

The paddle-wheeler was a varnished wooden boat with a paddle wheel that wound up with a rubber band. When the band was released, the paddle turned, propelling the boat through the water. Until now, the paddle-wheeler had done all its sailing in the bathtub back in their London home, and Ian could hardly wait to try it on the pond.

Ian crouched down beside Ollie and showed her how the paddle worked and then explained that they were going to sail it on the pond. She was interested and followed him to the water's edge.

Elinor went too, thinking that, perhaps, she could wash Ollie now. It was a very muddy pond — but there was a lot of dirt on Ollie to deal with. However, she and Ian were playing so happily together that Elinor decided to postpone clean-up time until later.

When Andrew came back he reported that Aunt Grace was going to Kelso that afternoon to do some shopping. She had wanted to know what they would like for supper, and he had suggested stew.

"Stew!" said Elinor. "Who wants stew?"

"I was thinking about Mae," said Andrew.

"She's going to find our food strange, and maybe she'd like something familiar for the first meal."

"I hope Aunt Grace doesn't make stew like Muckle-mooth Meg did. Ian wouldn't eat it — he said he saw an eyeball in it. I think stew was a dumb idea."

"What would your great idea have been then?" Andrew challenged.

"Let's not quarrel," said Elinor. "What should we do until Aunt Grace leaves?"

"Ian and Ollie seem to be doing all right," said Andrew.

Ollie was actually laughing as she sent the little boat across the pond to Ian.

"We could climb that hill. From there we would have a view of the road and see when Aunt Grace leaves and we can watch Ian and Ollie, too."

They were out of breath when they reached the top and threw themselves down. The turf was sprinkled with tiny flowers — purple, blue, white, yellow — all of them different, and Elinor wished she could name them. She decided she would buy a flower book the first chance she got.

At last they saw Aunt Grace come out of the front door and go around behind the house. Then her old car emerged from the garage at an alarming speed and went tearing off erratically down the road.

"I hope she makes it all right," said Elinor.

"She's driven that road plenty of times without us worrying," said Andrew. "Come on, we've got to get that kid cleaned up."

Ollie was still playing happily, but when Elinor and Andrew approached, the frightened look returned to her eyes.

"You tell her to come, Ian," Elinor suggested.

"Come on, Mae," said Ian.

"You're to call her 'Ollie,'" said Andrew.

"You can sail my boat in the bathtub. That's what I do at home."

"Bathtub?" questioned Ollie.

"We'll show you," said Ian.

So they took her to the cottage. Poor Ollie! Her head was swiveling on her shoulders, and her eyes were wide with wonder. There were so many things in the cottage that she could not comprehend. After she had got over her first fright, the light switch fascinated her. She was terrified when Elinor turned on the faucet in the bathroom but was eventually persuaded to put her hand under the running water. They laughed at her surprise when she found that it was warm, and she laughed, too.

Elinor did a thorough job of washing her while Andrew and Ian waited in the sitting room. They became increasingly uneasy when Ollie began to shout and scream.

Elinor was shouting, too.

"Hold still!" she said. "No wonder you've got soap in your eyes. I have to get the shampoo out of your hair. I'm not going to drown you!"

Ollie's yelling became louder.

Several times Andrew thought he heard Aunt Grace's car and went nervously to the door. Thank goodness they hadn't attempted this when Aunt Grace was home.

At long last Ollie and Elinor emerged from the bathroom. Dressed in shorts and a T-shirt, socks and sandals, face clean and hair brushed smooth, the child looked exactly like Ollie. Even Mr. and Mrs. Elliot would not have doubted that this was their daughter. They might have wondered about Elinor, though. She, usually so neat and clean, appeared with her hair damply plastered across her red face, her pants rumpled, and her shirt streaked with dirt.

"I need a bath, too," she said. "But we used up all the hot water."

They spent the rest of the afternoon exploring the cottage with Ollie and explaining things to her. After the ordeal of the bath she seemed to accept the amenities of twentieth-century civilization quite matter-of-factly. She scarcely blinked when they turned on the television, and she was delighted with the pop-up toaster and hot, buttered toast. They toasted a whole loaf of bread in an effort to keep her entertained and then remembered they had left their shrimp-paste sandwiches up at the castle. Well, that was no loss!

When Aunt Grace returned, Ollie was so startled by the car that they were sure the game was up before it had even started, but Aunt Grace didn't notice anything amiss.

"What have you been doing all day?" she asked.

"We were mostly around the castle," said Elinor. "Do you need help with supper?"

"You and Andrew can do the vegetables," said Aunt Grace. "The little ones can watch television. It seems to me that there are children's programs on at this time of day — not that I watch them."

They were glad they had introduced Ollie to the TV set, but she got bored with it very quickly. It was too much outside her experience.

Ian found Ollie's doll, Amanda, and some

of its clothes, and Ollie spent a long time dressing and undressing it and cradling it in her arms. She was also fascinated by the mirror in the bedroom and sat talking quietly to her own reflection. The others worried about what Aunt Grace would think of Ollie's strange broad accent but she scarcely spoke in Aunt Grace's hearing. They, themselves, were getting used to her voice.

Supper did not go smoothly. Aunt Grace, for the most part, was prepared to accept the children as they were, but when Ollie picked up the stew in her fingers, she felt she had to reprimand her. And Elinor was frantic when Ollie wiped her gravy-soaked fingers in her hair. Then she bit into a potato and apparently did not like what she tasted, for she spat it out onto the tablecloth.

"Enough of that!" said Aunt Grace, taking away her plate and marching out into the kitchen. "No pudding for you, my girl!"

Ollie seemed to shrink in her chair and looked so hurt and frightened that Aunt Grace relented and offered her a piece of cake.

She liked the cake but, in cramming it into her mouth, she sent a shower of crumbs onto the carpet.

After supper, while Elinor and Andrew

were doing the dishes, Aunt Grace got out the vacuum cleaner. This was one twentieth-century marvel that they had neglected to show Ollie, and she watched Aunt Grace uncoil the cord with the fascination of someone watching an Indian snake charmer. She was quite unprepared for the roar of the engine when Aunt Grace flicked the switch, and when the bag began to swell, she ran screaming from the room.

Aunt Grace unplugged the cleaner and said, "Don't tell me that child is afraid of vacuum cleaners. I thought children outgrew that sort of fear in babyhood — especially these days when they are surrounded by gadgets."

Poor Ollie ran from the house and Elinor saw, from the kitchen window, that she was heading for the keep as fast as her sturdy little legs would take her. Abandoning the dishes, Elinor went running after her.

When Elinor reached the castle, the door stood open. They had forgotten to lock it after Ollie went in looking for Muckle-mooth Meg and Anna. There was no sign of Ollie now. Elinor felt her way up the dark stairs and found the child crouched by the empty hearth. She looked around when Elinor came in, and there were tears running down her face.

She turned away from Elinor and seemed to be examining a stone down near the floor, running her fingers over it.

"John the Carver made that face in the stone. He made it for me — to watch over me. Where is John the Carver now?"

Elinor looked at the stone and could just make out in the dim light the crudely carved shape of a man's face.

"I don't know," said Elinor gently. "Come on home. It's time for bed."

Ollie had worn herself out with her crying and allowed herself to be led back down the hill to the cottage. Elinor noticed that Aunt Grace gave Ollie rather a shrewd look and was a little disturbed when she said, "Seeking the solace of the tower walls, was she? I have done that myself."

Elinor and Ollie shared a little bedroom upstairs, under the sloping roof, and Ollie objected only a little when Elinor tucked her into bed. She fell asleep almost at once, cuddling the old battered bear that Ian had brought her.

Elinor stood there, looking down at Ollie, thinking back over the strange experience they had all shared. The little girl stirred in her sleep and then twisted a strand of hair around her index finger, just the way Ollie did when she was tired, and Elinor was suddenly reassured.

Tomorrow everything would be all right. Ollie would be herself again.

10

Elinor wakened early, and her first drowsy thought was that it was pleasant to be in a bed instead of under a fur robe on the floor. Then she looked over at Ollie and was suddenly fully awake. Ollie's bed was empty.

She ran through to the boys' room and shook Andrew awake.

"Ollie's gone! She's gone back!"

"What do you mean — gone back?" asked Andrew, sitting up in bed.

"She's not in our room. I'm afraid she must have gone back."

"Get dressed and we'll go and look for her," said Andrew, reaching for his clothes.

They left Ian sleeping and crept downstairs quietly, hoping not to disturb Aunt Grace. As they passed the sitting room door, Elinor glanced inside and then grabbed Andrew's arm and pointed. There was Ollie, curled up in front of the fireplace, sound asleep.

"She must have found a bed as uncomfortable as we found the floor," said Andrew.

Ollie wakened at the sound of Andrew's voice and looked up at them with the wild eyes of a frightened rabbit.

"Don't be scared, Ollie," said Elinor. "Everything is going to be all right."

But everything wasn't all right. It was a struggle to get Ollie dressed, and breakfast was a disaster. Ollie picked up her bowl of porridge and slurped it noisily into her mouth and ate scrambled eggs with her fingers.

"We've got to teach her some table manners," said Elinor when they had all escaped outside.

"How can we, with Aunt Grace there?" asked Andrew.

"There's lunch time," said Ian. "Aunt Grace doesn't mind if we take picnic lunches."

"That's it," said Andrew, warming to the

idea. "We'll have elaborate lunches with knives and forks and teach Ollie about our food and table manners."

"Who is going to make these elaborate lunches?" Elinor asked suspiciously.

"We all are," said Andrew. "Aunt Grace has an old Primus Stove in the kitchen. I bet she'd let us take it, and we could heat soup and beans and stuff like that."

"That's an elaborate lunch?" asked Elinor.

"Compared to fish-paste sandwiches — yes! We'll think up other things to cook. I'm sure Aunt Grace will let us."

Aunt Grace was quite helpful with the picnic supplies and food, perhaps because she, too, had been finding meals with Ollie an ordeal.

Andrew enjoyed operating the Primus Stove and proved to be the most daring cook. Ollie had a good appetite and was quite co-operative at meals. She was especially eager to sample any new dessert.

One lunch time Elinor giggled as she laid a napkin by each place and straightened the knives and forks which Ollie had thrown down rather haphazardly. "What would Mother and Dad say if they knew we spent our vacation practicing table manners!"

This threw them all into such a fit of

laughter that they rolled on the ground. Ollie landed right on the tablecloth, laughing harder than any of them, although she wasn't sure what the joke was all about.

But progress with Ollie was not without its setbacks. One of their worst experiences occurred about a week later on a trip to Kelso with Aunt Grace.

It began with the problem of reading.

"It's going to be rough taking her back to London," said Andrew one day.

"I don't know," Elinor said. "She trusts us now, and she learns very fast."

"But what about school?" said Andrew. "She won't have us, and she'll be expected to know what goes on. She was there last year. And you know about her reading. You know that she was a sensation at reading."

"We'll just have to teach her," said Elinor.

They tried, and she wasn't interested.

"It's the way we're going about it that's wrong," said Andrew. "We're using the old Ollie's books, and they are too hard for her. We need some of these easy readers. You know — Dick and Jane and Spot. We'll have to get Aunt Grace to take us to Kelso so that we can buy some."

"Whose money?" asked Ian.

"We'll share the cost," said Elinor.

"Not my money," said Ian. "I'm not going to buy dumb books with my money."

"We'll share," repeated Elinor.

They asked Aunt Grace if they could go along the next time she went to Kelso. Ollie was very excited at the prospect. This would be her first car ride, and they prepared her for it by letting her climb in and out of the car when it was in the garage and by showing her cars on the road.

But they hadn't prepared her enough, or they hadn't prepared her for Aunt Grace's driving. When Aunt Grace switched on the key and the car roared out of the garage, Ollie gave a shriek of fright and threw herself down on the floor. Fortunately she was in the back seat with Elinor and Ian, and Aunt Grace was only aware of a mild disturbance.

For once, Andrew was in complete sympathy with Ollie. It was all he could do not to hide on the floor, too. Sitting up there in the front seat beside Aunt Grace he felt especially vulnerable. Aunt Grace drove so fast that the hedges went by in a blur. The car rattled and creaked, and she took every corner wide. Whenever they met an oncoming vehicle, there was an exchange of strident horn blowing.

As they got closer to town the streets got busier, but Aunt Grace did not slow down. She headed right for the center of town and parked in the wide cobbled town square, bringing the car to a stop in a series of noisy jerks.

"I don't suppose you came to Kelso to buy groceries," said Aunt Grace. "So I'll let you go about your business, and I'll attend to mine."

They went to the bookstore first. Ollie was mildly interested in the picture books, and they decided to buy the first four in a reading series.

"We can each pay for one," said Andrew.

"Not me," said Ian. "I'm not spending my money on baby books!"

"You are too!" said Andrew, making a grab for Ian's money.

Ian began to cry, and the other customers in the shop frowned at them. One interfering lady told Andrew not to bully his little brother.

Andrew and Elinor did not guess that Ian was happier with a young sister who couldn't read. All his life he had heard his parents and teachers go on about Ollie and her reading, and it would serve them all right when they found out that Ollie couldn't read any better than he could. He certainly wasn't going to spend his pocket money on books that would turn Ollie into a reading prodigy. He kept his money tightly clenched in his fist.

"Let him have his way," said Elinor. "I'll buy the fourth book instead of getting the flower book I wanted. There doesn't seem to be time to learn the names of flowers, anyway."

They left the bookshop and Ian, quite calmly, offered to spend his money on ice cream cones for all of them, and they all recovered their tempers.

They caused another minor disturbance in the ice cream shop. When Ollie bit into her ice cream she shrieked with dismay because it was cold. However, after the first surprise, she enjoyed it. In common with the old Ollie, she loved anything sweet.

"Let's stay out of shops," said Elinor. "We'll just explore the town."

Kelso was an old town with narrow, cobbled streets that wound down into the open square in front of the Town Hall. They walked along one of the streets at random and found themselves in front of the ruins of the old Abbey. Andrew looked at it with rising excitement and interest. Surely this must have been the very place where he had stayed.

Before he could tell Elinor this, it became apparent that Ollie recognized the Abbey too.

"They've knocked it down," she said. "They've broken it! It's all broken!"

And she burst into tears. All the strain of coping with the noise, speed, and unexpectedness of the twentieth century caught up with poor little Ollie in that moment, and she began to roar and cry as she had never cried before. A crowd gathered. Among it was the woman who had reprimanded Andrew in the bookshop.

"Still bullying your little brother and sister," she said.

And someone else remarked on the behavior of today's children.

Today's children, indeed, thought Elinor.

Then Andrew noticed Aunt Grace pushing through the crowd. Ollie was so out of control that Andrew was relieved rather than otherwise when he saw Aunt Grace bearing down on them.

She knelt down and pulled Ollie close to her.

"There, there, child," she said. "What's wrong?"

"They've knocked it down! It was the fairest place."

"People destroy things they shouldn't," said Aunt Grace. "And things change with time. The ruin is lovely now, too. See how high the tower looks against the sky. Nothing stays the same, but sometimes we can keep enough so that we remember."

Ollie's sobs subsided. Aunt Grace wiped her eyes and nose with a lacy handkerchief.

"That was a frightful fuss," scolded Elinor, upset and embarrassed though most of the people were now leaving.

"Don't be angry with her," said Aunt Grace. "Most of us just accept what we see. To see what might have been — and what might be — that takes special insight."

The children were glad to reach home. Not just on account of Aunt Grace's driving. They were beginning to see that Ollie wasn't ready for crowds. More and more they worried about their return to London. The summer was slipping away. They hadn't got very far with reading lessons, though in other ways Ollie was making good progress.

They found a photograph album that had a picture of their parents' wedding and explained to Ollie that these were her Mother and Dad. She could name most of her relatives in the album, though baby pictures of Elinor and Ian confused her. They drew diagrams of their house in London and studied pictures of animals she would see at the zoo.

Andrew had no time to be bored.

11

At first Andrew had not wanted to talk about his adventures in the past, but after seeing the ruined Abbey in Kelso, he was suddenly quite willing to recall details of his visit there. Elinor and Ian loved to listen, but they deliberately excluded Ollie from these talks — not wanting to remind her too much of her life as Mae.

"I wonder if it really happened that way," said Elinor, after hearing the story of the battle. "King James being killed by his own gun, and all that."

"I'm sure it did," said Andrew. "We could

check that in a history book. But it's Cedric I think about most."

"And Ollie," said Elinor.

They also wondered if the adventure could ever happen again. They never went inside the castle on their own, although they liked to play near it, and they sometimes had to unlock the door for tourists and show them around. Ian, unknown to the others, often checked the key to make sure that the magic had not come back.

If they had the chance to use the key again, would they do it, they wondered? Elinor said no, but Andrew said that there was still the unsolved question of the identity of Ollie-Mae.

She was sitting near them, looking at the pictures in one of her books, when they had this discussion. She sat there, small, chubby, and blue-eyed, and they realized they were terribly fond of her. The child, whom they had played with all summer, was the one they knew and loved. Had they ever really known the Ollie who lived with them in London?

And surely Ollie was happy with them. They couldn't send her back to the drab life of the fifteenth century with Muckle-mooth Meg.

"And all that awful stew," said Ian. "She'd really miss cake and ice cream!"

Then it was the day before their parents were due to return. Aunt Grace suggested that they should all go for a picnic by car.

"Roxburgh Castle would be a good place," she said. "It's between the Tweed and Teviot rivers."

"Wouldn't that be rather dangerous for Ian and Ollie?" asked Andrew. He was remembering Ollie's reaction to Kelso Abbey, and he wanted to avoid upsetting her again.

"I don't think we need worry about the rivers," said Aunt Grace. "Ian and Ollie are responsible children. Such a change I've seen in Ollie this summer."

So Andrew had to agree to go. Besides, he was curious to see the castle himself. It had been so majestic.

They arranged themselves in Aunt Grace's car. They were braver about traveling now, and Andrew even enjoyed it a little. Ollie knelt on the back seat looking out the back window, waving to surprised drivers of the cars they overtook.

The car suddenly swerved to the edge of the road and lurched to a stop in a shallow ditch.

We've done it this time, thought Andrew, but Aunt Grace said cheerfully, "Here we are!" and climbed out.

The children got out, too, looking around in a bewildered way and asked simultaneously:

"Are we there?"

"Where's the castle?"

"Over the fence here," said Aunt Grace. "You take the basket, Andrew, and Elinor can bring the blanket. Look out for the barbed wire."

They climbed the fence and followed Aunt Grace up a very steep bank, which was overgrown with nettles and thistles.

"This is it," said Aunt Grace.

All that there was to see were a few sketchy remnants of a broken wall and some piles of stones and more nettles and thistles. Ian noticed a wagtail fly out from a hole in the wall and went scrambling up to see if he could find a nest.

"This is the castle?" asked Andrew, looking around in dismay. "What happened to it?"

"I think the Scots destroyed it themselves," Aunt Grace answered. "They were tired of the English occupying it and using it as a stronghold against them, so they knocked it down."

They climbed right to the top of the mound.

"It was a good site for a castle," she went one. "The Teviot on one side and the Tweed on the other. They say that King James — the second, would it be? — was killed by his own cannon, trying to take this castle. It would be just down there that he died."

She pointed to a wide field below.

Ollie listened with interest but without emotion. There was so little of the castle left that nothing stirred in her memory. Even Andrew had trouble visualizing this as the site of a great battle.

"After the King died, did they go on fighting?" he asked.

"I rather think they did. I think that was when they drove out the English."

"I'm so glad," said Andrew. "It would have been such a waste of life and effort if they hadn't."

Aunt Grace snorted. "All wars are a waste of life and effort," she said. "Don't tell me that because James II's side won, it justified the battle. He was just as dead as if he'd lost."

And Cedric, too, thought Andrew, but he was still glad that Cedric had been on the winning side.

* * *

Then it was the morning of their last day.

Ollie could now read the four books that they had bought for her, and they were trying to get her to work on something a little harder. This morning she wouldn't cooperate at all. Perhaps they had been pushing her too hard, but there was so little time.

Elinor and Andrew were sitting on the rock beside the castle door — a favorite place of theirs — and Ollie was supposed to be reading.

"I don't know that word," she said.

"You do so," said Elinor. "Come on, just one more page."

"I don't want to read any more!"

"You must!"

"I won't!"

Then they saw Ian coming running up the path. Even before he reached them, they knew he had something important to say.

"The key! The key!" he shouted. "It's shining again!"

And he held the key out for them to see. It lay in his hand, glowing and luminous.

"The magic is back," said Ian breathlessly.

"What should we do?" asked Andrew.

"We don't need to do anything," replied Elinor. "Ollie can nearly read. She's happy here. We can't let her go back."

"But what about the real Ollie?" said Ian. "Maybe Mae's tired of reading. I heard her say she didn't want to."

"*I* don't want to go back," said Elinor, looking at the key with terror. "Do you, Andrew?"

"We wouldn't need to stay so long," said Andrew, curiosity overcoming caution. "We could just take a quick look around."

"But we wouldn't necessarily find Ollie. We didn't before. And we might lose Mae. It's too big a risk," said Elinor.

"I think *she* should say," said Ian, looking at Ollie.

They all looked at her, knowing that above all else they wanted her to choose to be with them.

But Ollie-Mae took the shining key from Ian's outstretched hand, inserted it in the lock, turned it, and pushed open the door.

They followed her inside.

12

They followed Ollie up the dark stairs. Andrew stumbled on a loose stone.

"Watch out," he said to Ian behind him. "Some of these steps are cracking away."

Elinor came last. She was terribly frightened. The only reason she had come at all was because waiting behind would have been intolerable. But now she felt so sick and shivery that she wondered if she could even climb the stairs. She followed them past the first room, to the second floor, and then the third. Ollie-Mae seemed confident in her leadership. Elinor caught up with the other three when they stopped at the barred doorway of the top floor. They were peering down, and the mist swirled below them.

"The magic's working," whispered Ian. "One of us has to go."

How does he know that, Andrew wondered.

Ian looked at them, his eyes round and frightened and his face pale in the eerie light. Then he deliberately crawled between the bars and stepped out into the nothingness of the mist.

"He didn't want to do that," whispered Andrew. "He was scared."

"We'd better go down," said Elinor, but she made no move to go.

Then Ollie said, "Come on! We must find Ian."

They climbed down the long winding stairway. It seemed to take forever, and they had to go carefully because several of the steps were loose or broken.

At the bottom they were met by none other than Ian — their own Ian. He was dancing about with frustration as he said, "It didn't work! It didn't work! The castle is still old and empty, and there's no one else here."

"But you're still Ian," said Elinor, throwing her arms around him. "I was so afraid that we would find someone else. You were so brave!"

"Stop it," said Ian, wriggling free from Elinor's hug. "I'm all right."

"What do you think . . ." began Andrew, but he never finished what he was asking because he was interrupted by a voice from across the room.

"You have come back! Tell me that you have come back and that your voices are not just a mirage of my fevered brain."

The children swung around, more afraid than they had ever been before. They had come down the stairs, keyed up, expecting to find themselves involved in something outside their understanding, but nothing had happened. Now their guard was down. This sudden, cracked old voice froze them where they stood.

"Speak, speak to me," said the voice plaintively.

"Who are you?" asked Ian.

"Are you not one of my own people that you must ask that?"

Cautiously Ian, followed by the others, crossed the room toward the speaker. The light was dim, and she was huddled in the darkest corner, wrapped in a blanket. They could not make out her features, but she appeared to be small and very old.

"Who are you?" Ian asked again.

"I am Vianah, but I do not know your voices."

"I'm Ian and these are my sisters, Elinor and Ollie, and he's my brother, Andrew."

"Where are you from?"

"We live around here. We just dropped in, you might say," Ian added and giggled at his own joke.

Elinor was horrified. How could he make a silly joke when they were caught up in these incomprehensible happenings again?

"You are not one of my people?"

"I don't think so," answered Ian.

"Are you one that they went to find? Have you a message from my people?"

"No," said Ian.

"Let the others speak. I would know them, too."

Elinor couldn't think of anything to say, but Andrew asked, "Who are your people?"

"The people of Kelso, just beyond the woods."

What a reassuring sound — the people of Kelso.

"Where have they gone?" asked Elinor.

"I am very weak from want of food and very cold," complained the woman, and her voice was indeed hoarse and strained.

"Can we get you something?" Andrew

asked, but she did not answer. She just shrunk down into her blanket.

"Maybe we ought to do something for her," said Andrew. "We could light a fire. I've got matches with me," he added, feeling in his pocket.

"We'll need wood," said Ian.

"Let's all go and look for it," said Elinor. "We're going to stay together this time."

They went outside and looked around in dismay. Nothing was as it should be. They half expected to see the thatched huts by the lake, but neither the huts nor the lake were there. Nor was Aunt Grace's house. Finding firewood would be no problem, for most of the land as far as they could see was covered with thick forest.

"Look!" said Elinor. "The key is still in the door. We could just go home."

"But what about the old woman?" asked Andrew.

"You said we'd come, and then go right back. The old woman has nothing to do with us. It's Ollie we want — remember?"

"But don't you want to know more about all this?" asked Andrew, gesturing around the whole sweep of the countryside.

"You promised," wailed Elinor.

"All right," said Andrew. "Lock the door."

Elinor put her hand on the key, and even as she touched it she felt it begin to turn in her hand. But at the last second she thought of the old, old woman inside the castle and of how she needed their help. Instead of turning the key she jerked it from the lock, saying, "Maybe we should take it so that nobody else comes along and uses it before we are ready."

She looked around at the grinning faces of Andrew and Ian and Ollie.

"We'll stick together," Andrew assured her.

They went down to the forest and gathered twigs and broken branches.

"How are we going to chop this without a hatchet?" asked Elinor.

"We can drag back the big branches," said Andrew. "That's a huge fireplace. Ian and Ollie can take that pile of small stuff. We'll need it to get the fire going. You and I can take the branches."

They were very heavy, and Elinor stopped to rest. Looking around she asked, "What time in history do you suppose this is?" She asked the question as casually as if she were asking the time of day.

"I've been wondering," said Andrew. "It feels very long ago — all these forests. Britain was once covered with forests."

132

"Maybe we'll see dinosaurs," said Ian.

"Of course we won't — not if there are people."

"Sabre-toothed tigers?" he asked.

"You'll only scare yourself, asking questions like that," said Elinor impatiently.

When they reached the tower, Elinor pushed open the door and said, "It's funny. The door and the tower seem older than anything else around here. Part of the roof has caved in — did you notice that?"

They made a pile of small twigs and pine needles in the fireplace, and Andrew applied a match to them. The flame flickered and sparked as it consumed the dry needles. Carefully they added more twigs and finally got a good fire going. So intent were they on building the fire that they paid no attention to the old woman.

"There is a pile of logs here," said Andrew. "I suppose we can use them."

"I feel the warmth of your fire," the woman suddenly said. "Can you brew tea?"

"Do you have tea?" asked Elinor. "There's a pot here we could boil water in."

"My supply of food and drink are finished. They did not expect to be gone so long. But there is mint growing by the stream. Boil water and make some tea from the mint."

"I wonder if she means that stream by the

133

edge of the woods," said Andrew. "Let's go and see."

They went back down the hill and found a small stream.

"Is that mint?" asked Andrew.

"I'm not sure," said Elinor. "I should have bought that flower book."

"It smells like mint," said Andrew, crushing some leaves in his hand. "What do you suppose we do with it?"

"Just use it like tea leaves," suggested Elinor. "Even a drink of water would help her. I've heard that you die of thirst before you die of hunger."

They carried the heavy pot between them up the hill, sloshing water as they went. Ian and Ollie wanted to stay behind and play in the stream, but Elinor was still determined that they stay together.

"What do we make the tea in?" Elinor asked Vianah when the water finally boiled.

"My mug is somewhere here," she said, groping around. Ollie ran forward to help.

"It's pretty," said Ollie, holding the mug up in the dim light. It was of fine pottery, elegantly shaped and beautifully colored.

When they handed her the tea, Vianah took the cup and breathed in its fragrance. Then she sat in silence and drank it.

"Can we get you something to eat?" asked Elinor.

"You would need to go to Kelso for food. I have finished what they left with me here."

"Kelso?" asked Elinor and Andrew together.

"Do you know the way? I still do not understand where you came from if my people did not bring you here."

"Would we have to walk there?" asked Elinor.

"You go through the forest until you reach the river, and then you follow the river down to the town."

"What will we use for money?" Andrew asked.

"Money," repeated Vianah. "Where are you from that you ask about money?"

"Don't we have to buy the food?"

"Take what you need from the garden."

"But won't the people mind?"

"There will be no one there. I tell you my people have gone. I started out with them, but I was too old and blind for another journey. They left me here with food and firewood. But they have been gone too long. The food is gone, and the fire went out."

Ollie and Ian had crept closer to the old

woman as she talked, and Ollie curled up on the blanket beside her.

"Two of you go, and these two stay with me," she said, reaching out and embracing Ollie and Ian. "They can keep the fire going while you are gone."

"But we were going to keep together," said Elinor.

"Let us stay and look after Vianah," Ollie pleaded.

"It might be better if they stayed here," said Andrew. "It would take them forever to walk to Kelso. But it's up to you, Elinor."

Elinor looked at the two children sitting cozily beside the old woman as if they had known her for longer than an hour or so. Surely they would be all right, and at least Andrew wasn't going off without her again. She agreed that they could stay.

"Are you sure you know where we're going," Elinor worried when Andrew plunged into the forest.

"Only in a vague sort of way," he answered. "It's no use trying to visualize the road as we know it. It's better just to strike through the woods and hope that we find the river."

The trees in this part of the forest were predominately beech, and there was very little undergrowth. They would have made good time except that Elinor insisted on making elaborate signs so that they would be able to find their way back. When they reached the river they didn't need to leave signs, but the going was slower. They could not stay close to the river because the growth was too dense, yet if they went back into the woods they lost their way.

It was very quiet and green. Occasionally they disturbed a bird and near the river there was a profusion of flowers.

"I'll tell you what's missing here," said Andrew. "There are no paths or anything made by people. No roads, no signs, no litter."

"What do you expect in a forest?" asked Elinor.

"Think of the New Forest," said Andrew. "It's big but there are roads and signs and notices all over. Here there's just too much nature."

After a little, Elinor began to get a feel of what Andrew meant. It was as if nature had obliterated man. It was a great relief when they rounded a bend of the river and found that they were out of the woods and on the edge of a wide grassy plain. Sheep and goats were grazing in small fields marked off by wooden rail fences. Beyond were fields of grain and vegetables and then a cluster of neat little houses, some built of stone and some of wood. The roofs were of slate or thatch.

"Do you suppose this is Kelso?" Andrew asked.

"It's not the Kelso we know," said Elinor.

"And we haven't come far enough," said Andrew. "I think this is where the battle was fought."

"The battle?" asked Elinor.

"Where James II was killed."

"Oh, yes! I forgot you were there."

They drew closer to the little settlement, and the stillness and emptiness were more frightening than even a hostile greeting would have been.

"What should we do?" asked Elinor.

"Let's knock on this door and make sure there is no one around," suggested Andrew.

It was a low building of logs, and they noticed there was no glass in the windows. No one answered his knock.

"We didn't bring anything to carry food back in," said Elinor.

"Maybe we could see if there is anything in the house we could use," said Andrew. He was curious to see inside.

The door was not locked, and they pushed it open cautiously. They were surprised at the elegance and comfort of the furnishings. The walls were covered with pictures, almost all of abstract designs. Elinor could feel power and emotion radiating from these pictures, something she had never experienced in looking at a picture before. One, in particular, held her attention. It was of blues and grays, but as she looked at it, shapes emerged and took new forms. She felt that she could have gazed at the picture forever.

Andrew was more interested in the carved furniture and the open fireplace, and then he noticed the shelf of books. Some were ordinary books, rather dull looking, and others were rolls of parchment like the scrolls of long ago. He took one of these from the shelf and unrolled it and studied it for a while. Abruptly he let it spring back into its roll and thrust it back on the shelf.

"Let's get those vegetables," he said roughly. "We didn't come here to snoop."

"But the pictures," said Elinor. "Aren't they wonderful?"

"There's a basket we could use," said Andrew, taking a large wicker basket from a hook near the door. "Now, come on!"

Elinor was annoyed by Andrew's sudden change of manner. She didn't want to be hurried away from the curious, peaceful room. She felt that the room itself had something to give her. But Andrew was already pulling beans and peas from the vines in the first vegetable plot with quick, angry movements.

The room had certainly had a different effect on him!

"Are these plants with the white flowers potatoes?" she asked him.

"Potatoes?" Andrew asked sharply.

"What's wrong with potatoes? Shall I pull up a plant and see if they're ready?"

"All right. And these look like carrots over there."

They filled the basket with vegetables, and then Elinor noticed that there were fruit trees beyond the houses. She went over and was surprised to find that the trees were laden with ripe peaches. She hadn't known that peaches grew this far north. She stopped to pick some, although Andrew was impatient to be going.

"Come on, Elinor!" he shouted to her. "We've got to get back to Ian and Ollie."

"There's something wrong, isn't there?" she asked, but he went running ahead without answering, the heavy basket bumping against his legs.

When they finally reached the place where

they had to strike off through the woods, Elinor begged Andrew to stop and rest.

"All right," he answered and threw himself down on the ground.

"What's wrong, Andrew?" Elinor asked again.

"I'll tell you what's wrong," he said. "We're not in the past, Elinor. We're in the future. This is the twenty-second century."

Elinor was silent for a minute and then asked, "What's so bad about it being the future? Don't you think it's interesting?"

"Interesting!" shouted Andrew. "How can you say *interesting*? I said the twenty-second century."

"I heard you, and I said, 'What's so bad about that?'"

"But it's not the way it should be. Did you see these houses? I don't think they even had running water, let alone television or telephones. By the twenty-second century every house should have its own computers and robots and maybe people would talk by telepathy. They had nothing . . . nothing. . . ."

"It looked O.K. to me. I liked their pictures."

"Their pictures? What has that got to do with it?" broke in Andrew. "I'm serious. I don't want to see any more."

"What makes you so sure this *is* the future?"

"I looked at a scroll in that house and it was all about the great floods of a hundred years ago — in the middle of the twenty-first century," said Andrew. "And there have been other clues. Like the potatoes."

"The potatoes!" said Elinor in amazement.

"I think it was the sixteen hundreds before potatoes were grown here, so we couldn't be farther back in time than we were before."

"And the tower itself is a clue," suggested Elinor. "It's more dilapidated than in our time."

"Let's go! We must get back to Ollie and Ian. I don't like this."

"Aren't you curious to find out more?" asked Elinor.

But Andrew didn't answer. He just ran ahead through the dappled shade of the wood. In his hurry to get back, he kept missing the signs Elinor had left in the morning. They would have been hopelessly lost had they followed his lead.

13

After Elinor and Andrew left, Ian and Ollie
felt a great sense of peace and belonging, sitting in the shadowed corner of the room
beside the old woman, almost as if they had
known her for a long time. At first she
seemed to be asleep, but she stirred when a
log rolled forward in the hearth, shooting up
a spurt of yellow flame.

"I cannot see you with my eyes," she said,
"but let me touch you, so that I may know
you better."

She ran cool dry fingers over Ian's features
and smoothed his hair back from his brow
and then touched Ollie lightly.

"Tell me this place you come from. Where do you live?"

"I lived right here," said Ollie in a low voice. "But it seems very long ago. I slept by the fire, and we sang in the evenings. Old Anna used to tell us stories."

"We're staying at Smailholm Cottage with Aunt Grace," broke in Ian. "It isn't far from here. We're just staying there for the summer while Mum and Dad are in France. They flew there."

"Flew?" Vianah questioned him.

"I wish we could have gone in a plane, too, but Dad drove us up here. All the way from London."

"Tell me about Aunt Grace and the cottage."

"Aunt Grace is very old — but not as old as you," answered Ian, peering at her. "She drives really fast and honks at everyone. The first time Ollie went in the car, she was really scared and hid under the seat, but she's used to it now."

Ian rattled on, telling the old woman of their visits to Kelso and their picnics by the tower. Several times she interrupted him with questions, especially wanting to know more about Aunt Grace and the pond where they played and details of the tower.

"You talk of many things that belong to an age that is gone," she said at last. "Things that my people only know from writings and artifacts. Leave me, now, for you have given me much to think about."

"Can we go down to the stream?" Ian asked.

"Yes, but do not wander far."

Ollie would have liked to stay with the old woman, but Vianah said to her gently, "You go, too, child. I wish to be alone."

So Ollie followed Ian out into the bright sunshine and blinked as she looked around at the still unfamiliar scene. The woods closed in all around them, leaving bare only the rocky hillside on which the tower stood. Ian was already down by the stream that ran along the edge of the trees and was taking off his socks and shoes.

"It's really warm! There's fish in this stream. Big ones!"

The fish were three or four inches long and were darting about in a shallow place where the stream spread over a gravel bar.

For a long time the children played, making channels in the coarse sand and diverting the water into it. Then Ollie tired of playing and sat on a big stone watching Ian. He had chased some of the fish upstream to a place where the water had undercut the bank, and he was now trying to catch them. Ollie got up quietly and walked back to the tower.

Contrasted to the brightness outside, the tower was dim, and Ollie could only just see Vianah sitting deep in the corner, wrapped in her blanket.

"So you have come back," the old woman greeted her.

"I wanted to talk to you," whispered Ollie.

"Ah, yes," said Vianah with a low laugh. "It was the boy who did all the talking before, but I think that you have a story to tell me, too."

Ollie sat down beside Vianah and began to talk of her life in the keep. She spoke hesitantly, for her memories were like half-remembered snatches of a dream. And then she spoke more confidently of Ian and Elinor and Andrew and of how she was learning to read and of playing with the paddle-boat on the pond and keeping tadpoles in a jar and picnics by the tower wall.

The old woman listened, chuckling sometimes, and only occasionally stopped the flow of Ollie's chatter with a question.

When, at last, Ollie ran out of words, Vianah said, "You talk of things of long ago."

"It's not all long ago," Ollie tried to explain, but just then Ian came running in.

"I caught a fish," he said, "Look!"

And, remembering that Vianah could not see, he added, "Would you like to hold it? I caught it with my bare hands, and we'll cook it for your supper."

Vianah stretched out her hands and took the cold, slippery fish and said, "This will indeed make a fine supper. It will give new strength to these old bones of mine. Take it and wrap it in wet leaves to keep it fresh. And I think that if you go down to the edge of the woods you will find that Andrew and Elinor are on their way back from Kelso."

"Vianah," said Ollie, still unwilling to leave. "How do you mean 'things of long ago'?"

"These things you talk of — cars and planes and even the people — they are all things of long ago."

"That's what Elinor says about Meg and Anna and John the Carver. Sometimes I don't know where I belong." Ollie's voice trembled, and Vianah sensed the tears welling up in her eyes.

"You belong with those you love, and those who love you," Vianah answered gently.

And Ollie ran down the stairs confidently and out into the sunshine to meet Andrew and Elinor.

14

"We're nearly there," said Elinor. "I can see Ian and Ollie by the stream."

When Ian saw them he came running to meet them and shouted with great delight, "I caught a fish! It was under the bank and I caught it with my hands. We're going to cook it for Vianah. Come and see it!"

Secretly, Elinor thought the fish was rather small. But she said the right things, and Ian continued to dance around and explained again and again just how he had caught it and how nearly it had escaped from him.

"We're going to cook it for supper," he told them again.

"We're not cooking any supper," said Andrew. "We're going home."

"But she can't do it by herself," said Ian and then added in a low voice, "she's blind."

"We're going home. We've brought her food. She managed before we came, and she can manage again."

"She didn't manage before we came," protested Elinor. "We can't leave her."

"You're the one who didn't want to stay," said Andrew.

"Well, I do now. I'm not going home."

They argued a while longer, and Andrew finally gave in.

They washed the vegetables in the stream, and Andrew cut the potatoes and carrots into pieces with his pocket knife. They boiled them together in the cooking pot. Andrew cleaned the fish for Ian, and they put that in the pot, too.

"How will we eat it?" asked Elinor, looking at the soup steaming in the pot.

There was only Vianah's mug, so they took turns, serving Vianah first. The meal lasted a long time, and they were disappointed in the taste of the soup — it needed salt, for one thing — but Vianah seemed to like it and was obviously strengthened by it.

"Ian and Ollie have told me many things,"

she said as they sat around the fire, sharing the soup. "Strange, unaccountable things. But there will always be much that we cannot understand, no matter how much we know. Even in this age of progress there are truths we have not discovered."

"This age of progress!" interrupted Andrew loudly. "You mean the way you live now? That isn't progress. I saw your town!"

"You cannot judge the town apart from its people," said Vianah.

"But there is no electricity and no cars, no roads, nothing! You're back in the fourteen hundreds. Even then they had cannons."

"You are indeed a child of your own time, a child of the Technological Civilization. That was an interesting period of history, a great experiment."

"What do you mean?" asked Andrew.

"It was an age when machines and speed mattered more than people, more even than the world in which we live," said the old woman, pulling her blanket around her and drawing closer to the fire. "But I am not a historian. I have never studied your time — and there is much that is incomprehensible to those who have."

"What happened to it?" asked Elinor quietly. She was beginning to understand why Andrew had wanted to go home. In the little house in Kelso she had seen only beauty and felt peace. She had not thought about the chain of events that lay between her time and this.

"The machines and gadgets that were so important to you took too much energy to run. And too many people wanted them. There was no sharing, each man and each nation guarded his own. There were bad times — wars, famines, and destruction."

"How long ago was this?" Andrew asked.

"The wars and famine happened over a long period of time. Even two hundred years ago there were people in the world who were starving while some areas lived in plenty. It's hard for us to understand it now, but the areas where the Technological Society was at its peak created waste gases and pollutants that gradually changed the very climate and atmosphere of our planet. The whole world became warmer, and the ice caps at the north and south poles melted."

"And that caused the floods," said Andrew. "I read about that in a scroll in a house in Kelso. That's how I knew we were in the future."

"Yes, there were floods that destroyed the great coastal cities and the people fled inland and there was a period of famine and disease. There were earthquakes and fires, and the

151

crops that the people cultivated would not grow. We have few written records from those dark days. Books and papers tell us much of what happened before the floods. But I suppose that during the years when their civilization collapsed, the people were too busy searching for food and fighting disease to record these happenings. They were a people without vision and without hope — they simply gave up."

The children sat around the fire with grave faces. Even Ollie and Ian seemed to understand.

"Where did your people come from?" asked Elinor.

"We do not know the beginnings of our own people. We come from the south, and our first written records are of the long journey by sea of a band of people seeking the cool northlands. We are a peaceful people and strive to live in the world and not to conquer it. Our great fear is of repeating the mistakes of the past — though we have little chance to repeat them. The resources and reserves of energy that we would need to imitate your way of life are all gone."

"Was anything saved from our time?" asked Elinor.

"We use much from the past. We have no

machinery for extracting metals from the earth as you did, but we use what we find in the scrapheap of your civilization, and we have built on your knowledge and discoveries. People will depend on your feats for many ages to come.

"But our talk should not be of such solemn things. In the evening we always sing. Come, Ian, sing that song I heard you singing earlier!"

Elinor and Andrew wondered what Ian would sing. He didn't leave them in doubt for long, but cleared his throat and began:

> "This old man, he played one
> He played knick-knack on my thumb
> Knick knack, paddy wack
> Give the dog a bone,
> This old man came rolling home!"

"Ian!" said Elinor. "That's a silly song."

"Vianah asked me to sing it. She likes it. What do *you* want us to sing?"

Elinor wondered. She felt maybe a hymn, or even the national anthem, would be more appropriate, but Vianah didn't wait for Elinor to decide. She joined in Ian's song, singing the chorus, and he taught her all the verses. They sang other songs, most of them suggested by Ollie and Ian, until the sun went down. Then they lay on the floor and went to sleep. Even without blankets, Elinor felt warm and relaxed and happy. Yet here she was, spending another night in the keep.

They awoke early, and Andrew kindled the fire and made another pot of vegetable soup. They ate some of the peaches that Elinor had picked, and they were sweet and juicy.

"How long are we going to stay?" asked Andrew.

He no longer felt the urgent desire to get home, but he didn't want to have to make another trip to Kelso. That had been too disturbing.

"There's no point in staying here," he told the others. "We're eating all the food we brought for Vianah. It's better for us to go now."

"But we don't know when her people will return," said Ian.

"She'll have to take a chance," said Andrew. "We've done our best."

Ian and Elinor might have given in, but Ollie would not hear of going back. She began to cry when they spoke to her of it and then spent most of the day talking to Vianah.

So evening came, and Andrew was more restless than ever.

"Who are your people?" he asked Vianah,

as they shared yet another meal of soup. "And where have they gone?"

"They are the people of Kelso. We took the name from an old town and ruined castle farther down the river."

"It was an Abbey," said Elinor.

"Maybe. There are just a few stones left now."

"But where have they gone?" asked Andrew again, feeling that she was avoiding his question.

"Just before the time of the harvest, we go seeking the settlements of the north. There are so few of us, and we have so much to share, so we try to persuade the scattered people to join us. Perhaps this will be the year."

"It's the opposite of the raiding parties of the fourteen hundreds," said Elinor. "Sharing parties!"

"Our crops always grow well in this mild climate with the long hours of daylight. We spend much of our time on art and weaving and music and poetry. And we are interested in history and in the writings of the past. My people like to travel during the long days, searching for artifacts of the past. In some places huge buildings still stand, buildings full of books and papers. It is because of these artifacts that all the people go. There is much to see and much to bring back."

"I bet there's a lot that puzzles them," said Andrew. "Think if you found a telephone directory and settled down to read it!"

"Or math books," said Elinor. "Or even comic books!"

"There is much that you could explain to them," said Vianah. "But I have been thinking that you should leave before they return."

"Why?" asked Elinor in surprise.

"I have told you that my people want more to join us," Vianah answered slowly. "I am afraid that if they found you here they would not want to let you go. They have a great curiosity about many of the things they find, and the knowledge you have of your civilization would be so valuable to them that they might not let you return to where you really belong. They might hold you here against your will."

"We could just meet them and explain a few things," said Elinor.

"Yes!" said Andrew. "We would be experts and give lectures on the twentieth century!" At that moment he rather liked the idea, and he had become a little curious about Vianah's people.

But Vianah shook her head. "I am afraid

that if they met you, they would not be satisfied with only a few answers. They would
want you to become part of our time."

Elinor and Andrew felt a shiver of uneasi-
ness at this thought, and Elinor surrepti-
tiously fingered the key which was still in
her pocket.

"I am sorry that they cannot meet you,"
Vianah continued. "They see the people of
your time as grasping and thoughtless. They
see greed as the cause of the breakdown of
the Technological Civilization. But perhaps
we look at the remains of your civilization as
you, Andrew, looked at our town of Kelso.
Without the people, you miss the meaning
and the purpose. *You* have put my needs before yours. We thought that was only learned
recently, and I am not sure that my people
know it now, or I could let you stay."

During this conversation Ollie and Ian had
wandered outside. They came bursting
through the door, greatly excited.

"I think your people are coming!" they
shouted. "Come on, we must go and meet
them!"

"No!" said Vianah firmly. "If it is within
your power, you must leave here now."

The children looked at one another un-
certainly.

"I will come with you to the door."

Vianah stood up shakily and placed her hand on Elinor's shoulder. In all the time they had talked with Vianah, they had not seen her clearly. She had sat in the darkest corner. This had not mattered, for there was such love and friendship in her voice that they felt they knew her.

They walked toward the door. Elinor took the key from her pocket and it still glowed. They could see Vianah's people coming from the woods — tall, brown people, with black hair. Proud, fearless people. They sang as they walked.

The children turned to Vianah and gasped in surprise. She was little and old and her hair was white, her blind eyes blue, and all her features were exactly like those of Aunt Grace.

"Come with us," said Elinor. "You belong more to us than to them. Come with us, Vianah!"

The brown people had seen them and were running up to the keep with long easy strides.

"Come with us!" begged Elinor.

But Vianah only smiled and turned back inside the keep.

Ollie took the key from Elinor's hand. She pushed it into the lock and turned it.

15

The children blinked and looked around. A rabbit darted from the cover of its burrow, surprised by their sudden appearance. The sun was warm overhead. A man and woman, laden with binoculars, cameras, and bags, were struggling up the slope to the keep while their dog bounded ahead.

The children watched them.

When they were close enough to talk, the man said, "Your aunt, down there at the cottage, said that you children have the key to the tower and would show us around."

"That was quite a climb," said the woman breathlessly.

Andrew took the key from Ollie's hand. He was reassured to see that it was the old black key, and he put it in the door and unlocked it.

"It's dark in here," said the man. "I can't see a thing."

"There are stairs in the corner," said Ian. "You can see better in the room upstairs."

"More climbing," complained the woman, but she followed her husband up the stairs. The dog pushed ahead of her, almost causing her to trip. The children went up, too, in silence.

"Is this all there is to it?" asked the man looking around. "It's hardly worth the walk."

"You can climb higher," said Elinor.

"But what more would we see?" asked the woman. "We can see it all from here."

The man went over and peered up the wide chimney.

"Come on, Robert," said his wife. "Let's not waste any more time on this place. If we're going to see the Abbeys at Jedburgh and Dryburgh and Kelso, and Sir Walter Scott's house at Abbotsford today, then we'd better be on our way."

The dog investigated the corners of the room, sniffing and wagging its stumpy tail.

"You're right," the man answered. "Not

much to this place. Never was, I would imagine. We'd better push on."

Ollie said, "There's a picture of a man's head on a stone down here."

But the visitors were already groping their way back down the stairs, having brought with them to Smailholm Tower the interest and imagination they would take to all the other places on their tour. The children followed them outside and sat down, waiting for them to leave. The dog was digging down into a rabbit hole, and it took them a few minutes to persuade it to come, but at last they headed back down the hill.

"Not much to this place," Andrew mimicked.

"That's what they think!" said Elinor. And then, turning to Ollie, she asked, "Ollie, did you want to stay there? You liked Vianah, didn't you?"

"No, I didn't want to stay. I liked Vianah, but I didn't belong there."

"But we haven't found out where you really do belong," said Elinor.

"I belong here with you," said Ollie. "You're nice to me."

"But what about London?" asked Andrew.

"You never played with me there," said Ollie, pouting.

"Do you remember London?" asked Andrew and Elinor together.

"I remember you never played with me," said Ollie.

"But what else?"

"Lots of things."

"What things?" asked Elinor, feeling that they were on the edge of something.

"I want to go down and see Aunt Grace."

"Tell us about London first," said Elinor urgently. "What do you remember?"

"I told you — things."

"Tell us something more."

"We went to the zoo."

"But we've told you about that. Tell us something we haven't told you."

"You never played with me."

"Something else!"

"Leave her alone," said Ian. "We want to go and see Aunt Grace. Come on, Ollie!"

Ian and Ollie went scampering down the hill.

"Do you suppose she really does remember London?" asked Andrew.

"She sure sounds like Ollie," said Elinor. "Ollie used to say, 'You never let me play,' in that same sulky voice."

"And we never did include her much, did we? In a way, we didn't really know her.

Poor kid! I suppose she did feel left out sometimes."

"She had Ian to play with."

"I don't think he played with her either until we came up here," said Andrew. "But we should go down and see Aunt Grace, too. Wasn't it queer that Vianah looked just like her? That scared me as much as anything."

"You were scared most of the time," said Elinor.

"Weren't you?"

"I'd go back again. There was something I liked about it."

"Not me," said Andrew. "Anyway, we'll never have another chance. Mother and Dad come tonight, and we go home tomorrow. I wonder if Ollie does remember London."

Down at the cottage they found Aunt Grace kneeling in a flower border, carefully forking the soil around the roses. Ollie and Ian were picking zinnias.

"Takes a lot of work, roses," said Aunt Grace. "But they certainly repay you for the time you spend on them." Aunt Grace's roses bore out the truth of this. "A couple were looking for the key. Did you show them around?"

"They weren't all that interested," said

Elinor. "They had a lot of other places to see today."

Aunt Grace sniffed. "Aye, there's some like that. They look at a lot of places and never see anything. They never give any part of themselves when they look at these old places."

"And you," asked Elinor carefully. "Have you seen more?"

Aunt Grace looked at Elinor curiously but did not answer. Instead she rose stiffly from her knees, brushing the dirt off her thick stockings, and said, "It's time for lunch. You children will be hungry. That's a fine bunch of flowers, Ian and Ollie. Leave the rest to grow in the garden."

Elinor set the table, and Aunt Grace opened a tin of beans. She let Ollie make the toast.

"We'll save the cakes for tea when your parents get here," she said. "But there's a bit of gingerbread we can have just now."

When they were sitting around the table Aunt Grace said, "You'll be taking some happy memories back to London with you. Your father always found it hard to leave Smailholm at the end of the summer."

"It's funny to think of Dad playing here," said Elinor.

"Many children have played here," said

164

Aunt Grace. "Do you know that when Sir Walter Scott was a boy he spent a holiday here after he had been sick? I'm sure the tower walls spoke to him."

The children waited for her to go on.

"There's a story about his visit here. One night there was a terrible storm — lightning flashing, and thunder enough to wake up the dead. Walter Scott's nurse went up to his room to comfort him, thinking he might be frightened, but the lad wasn't there. She looked out the window and saw him, sitting on a rock up by the keep, wearing only his nightshirt.

"In a great state, she went running out to get him, and there he sat, watching the storm. Whenever there was an extra bright flash, the lad clapped his hands and cried, 'Bonny! Bonny! Do it again!' He thought the whole show was being put on for him."

"How long have *you* lived here?" asked Elinor.

"I first came here as a child," said Aunt Grace. "I had been ill, too, with scarlet fever, and my mother thought the country air might do me good. Smailholm Cottage belonged to my grandmother then, and I was sent to stay with her. I was no more than three or four years old.

"One day I wandered up to the tower — it

wasn't kept locked then — and I crept inside. I stayed there for a long time playing and fell asleep. I was asleep when they found me, and afterward they wondered if perhaps I had fallen from the doorway of one of the upper rooms because I was so hard to rouse. And when I did waken I didn't seem to know where I was. I didn't even recognize my own grandmother. I never really did regain much memory of my life before that time — just fragments of a dream. But that doesn't matter now. I have a lifetime of memories to look back on."

"The dream?" asked Elinor, scarcely above a whisper. "What do you remember about the dream?"

"It's so long ago, my dear. I remember tall, brown people with long black hair and singing voices. They tried to keep me there. They were kind to me, and I wanted to stay — but they weren't my own people. I had to come back."

The children sat silent, gazing at Aunt Grace with round eyes.

"The tower has always given me a special feeling," she said. "When Grandmother died, she left the cottage to me, and I moved in here. I love this place. The way the sun shines on the stone, the coots on the pond, the larks so free in the sky, and the extravagance of the blossom on the gorse in June. I've always been happy here."

After lunch the children went back outside. Ian and Ollie wanted to play with the paddle-boat on the pond on this, their last afternoon. Elinor and Andrew wanted to talk.

"What do you think of Aunt Grace's dream?" Andrew asked.

"I think she's been there, too." said Elinor. "And do you know what else? I think part of her lived on as Vianah and grew old there."

"That doesn't make sense," said Andrew.

"Does any of it?" asked Elinor. "Maybe Mae went on living in her time, too. It always bothered me that perhaps we stole Muckle-mooth Meg's child. She loved her, you know."

"I never really worried about that," confessed Andrew.

"We should really give Ollie her reading lesson this afternoon," said Elinor.

They went down to the pond where the younger children were playing. Ollie was not eager to read because it was her turn to sail the paddle-boat.

"Just one page," said Elinor.

Ollie took the book impatiently from Elinor

and read a whole page without stumbling on a single word.

"How did you manage that?" asked Andrew in amazement.

"Vianah helped me," said Ollie.

"Vianah? But she was blind, and you had no books there."

"We didn't read," said Ollie. "We just talked. She told me so many things that day."

"Tell us about it," said Andrew.

"Not now," Ollie said. "It's my turn with the paddle-boat, and Ian's still got it."

And she ran from them, yelling, "I get two turns, Ian! You've gone all around the pond!"

"That's something else that doesn't make sense — learning to read without a book to read from," said Andrew, watching Ollie as she ran splashing through the muddy water and grabbed the boat from Ian.

Their parents arrived early in the evening, and the children raced out to greet them. In the excitement Elinor and Andrew forgot to watch Ollie to see if she seemed to recognize them. She hugged and kissed them with the others.

"You've got to come and see the castle," said Ian.

"And it's my turn to unlock the door," said Ollie.

Mrs. Elliot laughed. "Listen to Ollie! I do believe she has picked up a Scottish accent while she's been here this summer. Just listen to her!"

"You unlocked it last time." said Ian.

"Then I get to carry the key!"

Later on, when the children were in bed, Mr. and Mrs. Elliot and Aunt Grace sat around the fire having a cup of tea.

"I told you it would be good for them," said Mr. Elliot. "Have you noticed how Andrew and Elinor look out for Ollie? There's a bond between them all that was never there before."

"They've learned to appreciate each other," said Mrs. Elliot.

"Perhaps they have learned more than that," said Aunt Grace.

Smailholm Tower

Smailholm Tower stands rigid and alone, solid on an outcrop of rock, a blunt finger pointing toward the sky. It was made by man yet belongs to the landscape as much as the trees, the grass, the very rocks out of which it seems to grow. A small spring-fed pond below the tower is drying up and becoming choked with weeds and rushes, as if to emphasize that the things of nature slowly change while this man-made tower defies the passing centuries.

It is a Scottish Border Keep and was built in days when stout walls were defense against the enemy. A heavy metal-studded door of oak opens into a large, rectangular room where, long ago, the laird used to drive his cattle to keep them safe from marauding enemies. In less troubled times this bottom room served as a storeroom. The ceiling, which is still intact, is made of stone and earth and forms the floor of the main room above.

A spiral staircase, winding up within the thickness of the south-east wall, leads to this main room. There were once three rooms, one above the other, but the wooden floors have long since rotted away. Now the tower is an empty shell, tall and narrow, covered over by a roof of stone. Empty fireplaces and doorways high in the walls show where these rooms have been. The spiral staircase still leads to the upper floors, but the doorways are barred with stout iron rods.

The tower was built of the same gray, granite stone that thrusts through the thin coat of turf on the hillside. But the cornerstones are of red sandstone, and they were carefully cut and placed so that they form a symmetrical pattern down the tall, straight sides of the tower. Inside, too, sandstone was used to finish the stone seats in the window embrasures and in niches in the walls designed for candles. Simple touches, but they show that the tower was designed and built with pride. Over the fireplace is an arch of interlocking stones; and the square bottom stones, on the level of the floor, are crudely carved. One is etched into the shape of a man's head, and the other bears a pattern of intertwining leaves.

The tower stands, a silent witness to the march of time. It sheltered our forefathers long ago, providing them with a home and sanctuary from their enemies. Children grew up in the shadows of its walls. Today, it is a pleasant, peaceful place to picnic and play among the empty ruins. And it will still stand when our knowledge and skills are but a chapter in the course of the history of man.